ALL NIGHT LONG

MICHAEL LISTER

PULPWOOD PRESS

Books by Michael Lister

(John Jordan Novels)
Power in the Blood
Blood of the Lamb
The Body and the Blood
Double Exposure
Blood Sacrifice
Rivers to Blood
Burnt Offerings
Innocent Blood
(Special Introduction by Michael Connelly)
Separation Anxiety
Blood Money
Blood Moon
Thunder Beach
Blood Cries
A Certain Retribution
Blood Oath
Blood Work
Cold Blood
Blood Betrayal
Blood Shot
Blood Ties
Blood Stone
Blood Trail
Bloodshed

Blue Blood
And the Sea Became Blood
The Blood-Dimmed Tide
Blood and Sand
A John Jordan Christmas
Blood Lure
Blood Pathogen
Beneath a Blood-Red Sky
Out for Blood
What Child is This?
Blood Reckoning

(Burke and Blade Mystery Thrillers)
The Night Of
The Night in Question
All Night Long

(Jimmy Riley Novels)
The Girl Who Said Goodbye
The Girl in the Grave
The Girl at the End of the Long Dark Night
The Girl Who Cried Blood Tears
The Girl Who Blew Up the World

(Merrick McKnight / Reggie Summers Novels)
Thunder Beach
A Certain Retribution
Blood Oath
Blood Shot

(Remington James Novels)
Double Exposure
(includes intro by Michael Connelly)
Separation Anxiety
Blood Shot

(Sam Michaels / Daniel Davis Novels)
Burnt Offerings
Blood Oath

<u>Cold Blood</u>
<u>Blood Shot</u>

(Love Stories)
<u>Carrie's Gift</u>

(Short Story Collections)
North Florida Noir
Florida Heat Wave
Delta Blues
Another Quiet Night in Desperation

(The Meaning Series)
<u>Meaning Every Moment</u>
<u>The Meaning of Life in Movies</u>

Sign up for Michael's newsletter by clicking <u>here</u> or go to
www.MichaelLister.com and receive a free book.

For McKenna and Rylee
My extraordinarily lovely and loving nieces.

SERIES SALE

For a limited time the entire John Jordan series is on sale!

CLICK HERE to complete your series for the best price EVER!

JOHN JORDAN AUDIOBOOKS

Most of the John Jordan mystery thrillers are available on audiobook — and all will be soon.

CLICK HERE for more information and audiobook samples.

1

There's not a day that goes by that I don't think about Kaylee.

Each day holds something that calls to mind her calmness and kindness, her sweetness and joy, but I'd think about her even if it didn't.

Every case we work reminds me of her case, of *the* case of cases, the one that matters the most to us, the one case we've yet to solve.

Kaylee Walsh, my foster sister, went missing when she was twenty-one and I was a kid. Her disappearance haunts me like no other. It's the case that keeps me up nights, the reason I do what I do. Her mysterious vanishing is the reason I became a finder of lost souls—a private investigator specializing in missing persons cases.

When Kaylee was just a junior at the University of Florida in Gainesville, for reasons no one has ever discovered, she lied to her professors about a family emergency and left campus without telling anyone. Later that night, on a flat stretch of rural road in Georgia, she ran off the highway into a ditch. Then, even with witnesses watching from a nearby farmhouse, in the span of some six minutes, she disappeared off the face of the earth. Vanished into thin air. Without a trace. Never to be seen again. That was ten long years ago, and we're no closer to finding her now than when she first went missing.

Every client who comes through our door is me—a loved one who has lost someone and who is themselves lost, stunned at the random, capricious nature of existence, gutted by guilt and grief, hollowed out by questions with no answers, driven mad by relentless, obsessive wonderings and what ifs.

I always think of Kaylee, but I wonder if I'm thinking of her even more these days because I fear I'm about to lose another sister.

Blade, my sister and partner and person, is under investigation in connection with the disappearance of Chrissy Violet, a troubled young woman and the ex of Blade's girlfriend, Cindi Rush, who abducted the two women before going missing herself.

I'm sitting alone in our office sipping coffee and indulging such thoughts when Ben taps on my open door and walks in.

Ben Simmons looks like an attorney. He's a thin, smallish late-twenties man with dark, stylishly short hair and a boyish face. He's dressed conservatively in an expensive black suit, gray shirt and tie, and shoes that cost more than my entire wardrobe.

Ben is one of our fellow fosters and the reason we have such a nice office inside the law firm of Lewinsky, Clemons, Bradley, and Sykes located in an opulent new building on 15th Street near St. Andrews. Ben had arranged it so we could barter skip traces and defense investigator work for the use of the posh office we occupy.

Ben is followed by a late-twenties white man with pale, slightly sunburned skin, closely cropped light brown hair, and intense blue eyes.

"This is Liam Dunn," Ben says. "He's a client of mine who needs some investigative work done. Where's Blade?"

I shrug. "Not in yet."

He gets the same worried look I have, but it quickly vanquishes from his face.

Ben and Liam take the two seats in front of my desk.

"We have every indication that Liam is going to be indicted for the disappearance of his fiancé, Brooklyn Hill."

He tosses a file folder on my desk, and I open it.

On the left side is what looks like a professional headshot of the missing woman, and I wonder if she's an actress or model. She's striking, especially her brilliant blue eyes beneath her dark hair and the way her dark hair frames porcelain-like skin of her pale, roundish face.

On the right side is a summary of the case and a series of newspaper clippings.

About a year ago, during a bachelorette weekend, Brooklyn Hill, walked into a bar with her bridesmaids during an extended pub crawl on Panama City Beach and never walked out again. The case has gotten a good bit of attention and noto-riety because of the baffling nature of Brooklyn's disappearance and how attractive and sympathetic she was.

Ben says, "Ideally, we'd like to find out what happened to her and who's responsible before the indictment is handed down, but failing that we'd need help getting ready for the trial —finding other possible suspects, tracking down witnesses, establishing alibis. That sort of thing."

"My attorney here keeps telling me to quit saying this," Liam says, nodding toward Ben, "but I want you to know that I'm innocent. I love Brook like I've never loved anyone. All I've ever wanted to do is take care of her and protect her. I should've never let her go out on that silly bachelorette party thing—or I should've gone to keep an eye on her. I'll do anything I can to find her. Anything."

Ben says, "Liam is a highly decorated and well-respected state trooper. He has an alibi for the night Brooklyn went missing. But the DA is feeling pressure to do something, so . . . he's who they're going after. They should've never even convened a grand jury with what they have. No body. No evidence. No nothing."

It's a case that's baffling in the way that Kaylee's case is baffling—a truly inexplicable mystery that defies logic, reason, and even the laws of nature. Brooklyn and her bridesmaids walk into Jungle Jim's, a crowded club on the beach and the final stop on their pub crawl, and, about an hour later at closing time, as everyone is exiting Brooklyn is nowhere to be found.

Every entrance and exit of the club is covered by surveillance cameras. Everyone who entered the club that night, including Brooklyn, is captured going in. Everyone who exited the club that night, which includes everyone but Brooklyn, is captured coming out. Brooklyn never left Jungle Jim's, but she's no longer inside—a thorough search, which included both scent and cadaver dogs proves that. So where is she? What happened to her? How is any of this even possible?

"Local law enforcement called in FDLE and even a consultant from the FBI," Ben says. "They've come up with exactly nothing. And they've long since stopped trying to explain it. They just want to arrest someone."

"*Me*," Liam says.

I nod slowly and think about it.

"Ben keeps telling me they have no case," Liam says, "that I'll never be convicted on what they have, but I'm not worried about that. All I care about is finding Brook. Can you do that? Ben says you and your partner are the best, but . . . all these other agencies haven't come up with anything. I don't care what it costs. I've just sold my house to cover the costs. I'll pay whatever it takes, but I want results."

He indicates the luxurious office we occupy, which had been furnished and decorated by a young, indulged female attorney from a monied family who left everything when she moved on to bigger and better things.

"I'm not impressed by fancy offices or reputations. I only care about results. Brook means everything in the world to me. Everything. Please tell me you can find her."

Blade walks into the office and says, "*We* can find her."

2

————

"So what's the deal with this little runaway bride?" Blade says.

Liam is gone, and she has taken his seat next to Ben.

Resembling a slightly undersized collegiate linebacker, she is thick and muscular, a powerful physique with a low center of gravity. As usual she's wearing a pair of black ninja webbing drop-crotch multi-strap cargo pants, matte black greasy leather boots, a black retro leather biker jacket with lots of silver-toned zippers and a buckle belt at the bottom, a plain black tee fitted to her powerful frame, and a black snapback hat worn backward. She looks like a lez version of Black Panther.

Ben says, "That's what you two have to find out."

"Where have you been?" I ask.

"Playin' another round of cops and niggers with Bob Kirkland," she says.

Ben says, "I told you not to talk to him without me being present."

"I got this," she says. "Tell me about this new case."

Ben shakes his head and frowns, but does as she says. "Girl walks into a bar and never walks out again. Cameras everywhere. Big crowd. Impossible for her to just vanish, but that's exactly what she did."

"Glitch in the surveillance system," Blade says.

He shakes his head. "Every exit is covered. Every second is accounted for. And the other buildings in the area have security cameras of their own. Everyone who left the bar that night has been accounted for—from multiple angles. She wasn't one of them. She did not come out of the bar."

"Then she's still inside," she says.

"It has been thoroughly searched," he says. "I mean thoroughly and completely. Floors. Walls. Every nook and cranny. Search and cadaver dogs. She's not in there."

"So she didn't come out, but she's not still inside," she says.

"If you two solve this one you will be the undisputed champs."

"We already that."

"I'm serious."

"So am I."

"This one's like no other," he says. "You know I'm a true crime junkie. I know of a lot of mysterious missing persons cases, but none quite like this one. I'm not even askin' y'all to solve it. Don't expect that. It'd be great for her family, of course, but . . . I just need some alternative suspects, some reasonable-doubt material."

"We gonna solve it," she says.

I say, "How good is his alibi?"

He shrugs and frowns. "Not great. Friend of his says he was with him the whole time."

"He really sell his house to—"

"To find her," Ben says. "Yeah. He's serious about it."

"Hope you got a big fat retainer," Blade says to me.

Ben says, "I'm sure he did it for his defense fund too, but . . . I really think he's innocent. Seems genuinely perplexed and extremely distraught. I've represented a lot of guilty clients—"

"Like Blade, for example," I say.

She laughs.

"That's the job," Ben says. "And I don't mind it, but . . . I don't think he's one of them."

"Do you have any theories?" I ask.

"You heard of the backroom?"

I shake my head.

"It's like there are these backrooms—sort of like in the Matrix—that people can slip into and get stuck."

Of all our brothers and sisters, Ben is the most straight-edged and the least woo-woo. There's no way he subscribes to a theory like this one.

Blade says, "Like some other dimension and shit?"

"Yeah. I don't believe it, of course, but . . . if anything was going to make me believe in a supernatural explanation this case would."

Blade says, "I sure as shit hope you not gonna use the alien abduction defense in my case."

He laughs. "I'm just pointing out that this case is . . . I don't know. I'm tellin' you there's nothing like it. You'll find all manner of crazy conspiracy theories online, but . . . no, I don't have a working theory. Very, very few people vanish without a trace."

"But some do," I say. "Kaylee did."

"And," Blade says, "it wasn't because she got sucked into a different dimension."

Ben looks at her. "I know you think that because they haven't found Chrissy Violet's body they won't prosecute, but . . . look at this one. They've got no nothing—including a body—and they've convened a grand jury and they will indict."

"Well, maybe after we find Brooklyn and figure out who's behind her disappearance," she says, "we'll do the same in Chrissy's case."

3

———————

"How bad's the heat?" I ask.

She knows I'm referring to the investigation into Chrissy Violet's disappearance and her involvement.

"Bearable," Blade says.

She and I are in her vehicle driving out to Jungle Jim's.

It's a bright, clear early November day, the offseason traffic on 98 light and moving toward the beach at a steady clip.

"Anything I can do?" I ask.

She shrugs.

I can tell by her demeanor that she's worried.

All this time we've been thinking I'd be going back to prison —if I violate my probation I'll be sent back to serve out the remainder of my sentence. It never occurred to me that Blade might be the one to involuntarily leave our agency.

"Are they pressuring Rush just as much?" I ask.

Cindi Rush, Blade's current girlfriend and Chrissy's ex, is a talented local musician with an incredible voice, a young pixie with pink hair who seems as mentally fragile as she is physically—an assessment I hope I'm wrong about.

She nods. "More."

Rush is the chink in Blade's armor, the place where the cops will get in and deliver the fatal stab.

"How's she holding up?"

"She's pretty shaky."

"How much does she know? How much damage can she do?"

"Not that much."

Why'd she have to take Chrissy out? Why couldn't she have exacted her revenge in another, less precarious and potentially costly way? Why didn't I try even harder to stop her? I had been incapacitated by a taser at the time and felt like I had done all I could do, but now wish I could've somehow done more.

"You've never told me exactly what you did," I say.

"And I never will. Don't have to lie if you don't know anything."

"Thought we told each other everything."

"You got enough to deal with without this," she says. "You begged me not to do it. Tried to stop me. Told me Rush would be a problem. This all on me. Not involving you. Let's just see if we can find this missing white girl while I'm still a free woman of color."

4

Jungle Jim's is a large club on the second story of an entertainment complex on Front Beach Road not far from where the old Miracle Strip Amusement Park used to be. The two storefronts below it are occupied by a tattoo parlor and a touristy t-shirt and trinkets shop. Across the street from it, on the beach side of the highway, is a massive multi-story hotel. To the west of Jungle Jim's building is an arcade with a go-cart track, bumper boats, a haunted house, and mini golf. To the east is a Wendy's burger joint.

Harley Chandler, a mid-twenties young woman with a mouthful of large, bright white teeth and a headful of long, thick blond hair, is waiting for us out front. She's thin without looking emaciated and well put together without being pretty.

"Y'all are the ones who found that missing kid," she says, as we shake hands. "I recognize y'all. Sure hope y'all can find Brook. This has been the most . . . Anyway, I'm the one who coordinated everything with the group." She unlocks the door and leads us in. "I'm the hostess, but I mainly work with parties and just making sure everything runs smoothly and everyone has a good time."

Inside, we climb up an escalator that's off to the double doors of Jungle Jim's.

"Have y'all watched the videos of them coming in?" she asks, pointing to the surveillance camera mounted to the ceiling above the escalator. "Clearly shows them all coming back in."

"Back in?" I ask.

"They were here earlier in the night. They were doing an elaborate pub crawl. We didn't expect them to come back. They didn't have reservations or anything. The first time they had an entire section with bottle service and various amenities. When they came back the second time . . . it was less than an hour until close. They were tired and drunk. Happens a lot—where you know the night is over but you're still out trying to recapture some of the magic from earlier. They weren't fall-down drunk—just sort of subdued and a little unsteady. They were a good group. I work with a lot of bachelorette parties, and there are some real monsters out there, but these girls . . . they were sweet and gracious for the most part."

Jungle Jim's is decorated in a jungle motif with a large round bar in the center of the enormous open room, a stage and dance floor to the left, roped-off VIP sections with plush leather couches along the other walls.

"None of us can figure out how she just vanished like that," Harley says. "And we've tried. There are a ton of cameras in here and every exit is covered. Only place not covered is inside the bathrooms."

"Are there windows or doors in the bathrooms?"

"Very high, narrow windows," she says. "I'll show you."

She leads us over to the women's restroom.

As we enter, the lights blink on.

Beneath a wood plank ceiling, a dark ceramic tile floor, black granite countertops, and gold fixtures give the space an elegance that club restrooms don't normally have. On the left is a row of flat black stalls and on the right a row of sinks. Between them is an intricate pattern in the tile that pulls together all the muted colors in the room. Behind the sinks are large, spotless, well-lit mirrors.

She points to a one-foot square window that doesn't open about ten feet up the far wall.

"It would take a very tall ladder just to get up to it, and you'd have to break it—it doesn't open. Then you'd have to fall about thirty feet to the pavement and probably break your legs. And the outside cameras would capture you doing it."

We step out of the bathroom back into the bar.

"What other exits are there?" I ask.

"Service elevator in the back behind the stage for bands to load in and out and for deliveries. Leads to a loading bay on the first floor, but it's completely covered by cameras—the hallway, the elevator, the loading dock, the exterior of the building. Come on. I'll show you."

She leads us across the large club floor, around cocktail tables and high bar stools with backs to a door at the right of the stage.

"Was there a band that night?" I ask.

She shakes her head. "DJ."

A small, dim hallway leads to a service elevator beneath an illuminated Exit sign. We take it and then take the elevator down to the loading bay.

"Did he have equipment cases large enough for her to fit in?"

"I don't think so, but you can check the videos and talk to him. He's cooperated with the police. And even if he did have a case large enough for a person, he'd have had to leave equipment behind in order to fit her in it, and he didn't do that. Plus he was being watched and videoed the entire time. I don't see how he could've done it."

We look around the loading bay for a few minutes, though

there's nothing much to see—a concrete loading dock with yellow bollard parking posts, beyond which is a large metal roller door.

We take the elevator back up and walk out into the club.

"I truly believe every possibility has been exhausted," Harley says. "Not only by the police and employees, but for the past year we've had a steady stream of internet detectives showing up here with new theories thinking they're gonna be the ones to solve it."

"We're way behind," I say. "And we don't think we're gonna come up with something new. Just trying to get a feel for everything. Sorry to be asking such obvious and stupid questions."

"No problem. I keep thinking somebody's gonna come up with something that could explain it or she's just gonna show up. It's driving us crazy—especially Chase."

"Chase?"

"Stevenson. The owner. Do y'all know his story? His niece was beaten and raped at a club in Tampa. His whole thing was to design the safest club on the beach where if anything ever happened you'd be able to see it from every angle because of all the cameras. He hires the best bouncers and always has extra on duty—more than any place on the beach—and then something like this happens. It hasn't hurt business any—just the opposite, but . . . we all wish it had never happened. If you can find her . . .we'd be more grateful to you than I could tell you."

"Oh, we gonna find her," Blade says. "We may be late and off to a slow start, but . . . we sure as shit gonna find her. Bet that."

5

___

"Why do the innocent suffer?" Chase Stevenson asks.

Blade, Harley, and I have just walked into his office, and these are his first words.

His office sits suspended high above his club—almost like a cloud, an illusion reinforced by the near-total whiteness of everything. White walls. White ceiling. White carpet. White furniture.

Sitting in an enormous white high-back office chair behind a huge white desk, Chase is wearing something like a white silk martial arts Gi. His pale, bald, misshapen head is large and overwhelms his smallish face. His teeth are too large and too plentiful for his smallish mouth and jut out at a sharp point.

"I guess we could ask the same about the guilty," he adds, "but we don't really care that the guilty suffer, do we? They deserve to suffer, but the innocent . . . their suffering is so offensive somehow."

Everything he says has a slurpy too-wet sound to it.

"From all I can tell," he continues, "Brooklyn Hill was just such an innocent. And for whatever happened to her to happen at my club . . . it offends me no end. Anything you need to find her, to find out what happened to her . . . you have but to ask. Just let young Harley here know."

"Thanks," I say.

"Were you here the night Brooklyn vanished?" Blade asks.

Chase Stevenson smiles and somehow managed not to cut his lips. "My dear . . . I'm always here."

"Did you talk to her?"

"Oh," he says with another odd and awkward smile, "I see your confusion. By here I meant literally here. Up here on my cloud nine, not down there with the masses . . . and all their . . . malignant little microbes."

Blade starts to say something else, but Chase raises his hand.

"Run along now," he says. "Daddy's got work to do."

Harley grabs each of us by the elbow and begins ushering us out, hurrying us along.

"And Alix," he says, using Blade's legal name, though she hadn't given it to him, "if you ever want to come back alone sometime . . . feel free. Love the contrast you would provide." Not only is Blade black, but everything she had on is also black. "Harley will give you my private number. Just guard it for me, okay? And call me sometime. An enchanted evening awaits you."

"Sorry, but I play for the other team," Blade says.

"Oh, you misunderstand me," he says, smiling lasciviously. "I didn't mean for sex. I have no interest in erotic entanglements."

6

———

"**M**y dad's a huge *To Kill a Mockingbird* fan," Harper Leigh Gallagher is saying.

"Who isn't?" I say.

"True," she says, "but not many people name their daughters after it."

"I don't know," I say. "There are an awful lot of *Scouts* in the world."

"I guess that's true. At least Mom made him change the spelling of *Lee*."

Harper Leigh Gallagher was Brooklyn Hill's best friend. She's an athletic young woman who, like many of the bridesmaids, could be Brook's sister. Thought not as striking as Brook, she also has dark hair, bright blue eyes, pale skin, and a roundish face.

We're meeting with her in her little boutique art gallery in downtown Panama City. The space, on Harrison, is small and narrow and mostly features her own work—beachy watercolors of the untalented variety.

Fortunately for her, she's married to an engineer from a

wealthy family and does not rely upon her art to make ends meet.

"I'll never get over what happened," she says. "It haunts me like nothing ever has. It's . . . so . . . surreal. I've driven myself crazy trying to figure out what happened to her and how and who. It . . . doesn't seem real. And the timing . . . she was on the verge of actual happiness . . . and then . . . this."

"Was she not happy before?" I ask.

She shrugs and scrunches up the skin of her smooth face. "I just meant . . . to be honest . . . she wasn't. She hadn't had an easy life. That's an understatement. Anyway, she was such a sweetheart and deserved all the happiness she was getting— and then for it to be snatched away from her like that . . . It's too cruel. Anyway . . . I can take you through the night and tell you what happened and everything."

"I'd like to hear more about Brooklyn first," I say.

She shakes her head and crinkles up her face again. "I'm not comfortable saying anything else about all that. Said more than I should have already. Not my place."

"A lot of times the key to finding a missing person is in their past," I say.

"I'm sure there are others who can tell you about all that," she says. "I just can't."

"Okay. Then tell us about that night."

"It was . . . perfect. One of those magical nights that happen once in . . . I don't know . . . a blue moon. Not often. That's for sure. And it made me so happy for Brook. I don't know how many bachelorette parties y'all've been to—"

"Not many," Blade and I say in unison.

"The thing is . . . a thousand things have to go right for them to be good and only one thing to go wrong to ruin everything. And I'm tellin' you . . . everything and I mean everything went just right. The first thing to remember is that though the bridesmaids all have a connection to the bride they usually don't have a connection to each other. So many personalities thrown together. Virtual or actual strangers. You never know what you're going to get. But these were all really good girls. The best, really. All there for the same reason—to give Brook the best night ever. And we did. Right up until she disappeared."

"Small glitch," Blade says.

"And it wasn't just that bridesmaids all got along, but . . . everything ran so smoothly and worked out just right. Everywhere we went, everyone celebrated Brook. Everybody upgraded us and gave us extra and did little touches that made all the difference. And . . . this is bigger than you might think . . . there were no other bachelorette parties out that night. So Brook didn't have to share any of the attention. It was . . . perfect."

"Sounds like it," I say.

"We couldn't know what was going to happen, but if you had said this will be your last night together so make it a good one . . . we couldn't've made it any better."

"Did it feel like a last night together?" I ask. "Did Brooklyn give any indication that—"

"No. Nothing like it. Just the opposite. We all just thought it was the perfect beginning to a bachelorette weekend."

"So it was just the first night?" Blade asks. "There was more?"

"An entire long weekend of activities, yes."

"What did y'all think when it was closing time and you couldn't find her?" I ask.

"We were mostly confused. We were all pretty drunk and not processing things too quickly. We searched for her, thought maybe she got sick or just sat down somewhere. When we couldn't find her anywhere we thought maybe she was in the car. When she wasn't there we thought maybe she did an Irish goodbye and took an Uber back to the hotel or to see Liam. We called her phone like a thousand times. We didn't really get worried until we got back to the room and she wasn't there and when we called Liam and he said she wasn't with him."

"Do you think he could've had something to do with it?" I ask.

"*Liam*?" she asks, her voice rising in pitch and volume. "No way. He's one of the good guys. Have you met him yet? He's the salt of the earth, Southern gentleman type. He could never hurt anyone—especially a woman, especially Brook. He's the kind of guy who might bore you to death or smother you with too much attention, probably has too many rules you have to live by, but he's never ever *ever* gonna hurt you."

"You known him a long time?" Blade asks.

"Not too long."

"'Cause you seem awful damn certain."

"If I thought for one second he was capable of hurting Brook . . . He's just not. But don't take my word for it. Take a close look at him. Take a close look at all of us."

"Oh, we *will*," Blade says. "Bet that."

"Mind if I ask . . ." Harper says. "Why . . . do they call you Blade?"

"It's my weapon of choice."

Blade is never without a knife, and she often has several and a few hidden razor blades on her person at any given time. It began back in adolescence when we were being shuffled between group homes, state facilities, and foster care as a way of protecting herself from bullies and sexual predators, but it has evolved over the years.

"Any ideas what might have happened or who might be behind it?"

She shakes her head. "I wish I did. I've gone over and over it since it happened and just can't get any kind of handle on it. It's . . . I feel like it has broken my brain as well as my heart. I just know she's a completely innocent victim and whoever did it is an unimaginable monster. That's it. That's all I know."

"Why won't you talk about her past?" I ask.

"I don't know much about it," she says. "I just know it wasn't easy. If I knew something that had anything to do with what happened to her, I'd tell you. I just don't."

"Can you take us through that night?" I ask.

"I was thinking about that," she says. "Why don't the girls and I actually take you through it step by step. I could rent the same limo we had and we could go from place to place, show you everything, tell you what happened at each stop—it'd probably help jog our memories too."

7

———————

Alana, my four-year-old niece, and I are walking down Beck on our way back from getting tacos at Los Antojitos when I spot Clyde Broussard waiting for me on the sidewalk in front of the Publishing Museum.

He's an enormous black man—big in every way with both muscle and fat and huge hands that resemble antique weathered catcher's mitts.

He works security and enforcement for Logan Owens, the sexual predator who sent me to prison and who now has the means to send me back.

Clyde works for a bad guy but he's not one, and over the past few months he and I have formed an alliance of sorts to try to make the best out of the situation we find ourselves in.

Alana squeals when she sees him and runs over and hugs one of his huge legs.

He leans down and hugs her back, his giant mitt eclipsing her small back as he pats it.

"Clyde," I say.

"Burke," he says. "What, no hug?"

I pry Alana off his leg and says, "Give me a minute."

I lead Alana over to the Little Free Library at the south end of the building and find her a few tattered books. "Will you sit here and read this while I talk to Mr. Broussard for a minute?"

I keep Alana a few nights a week while her mom, my foster sister, Ashlynn, works.

She nods. "Then we get ice cream?"

And on nearly every one of those nights we get ice cream.

"Then we get ice cream," I say.

"With all the sprinkles?"

"With all the sprinkles."

I step back over to Clyde.

The humidity has finally dropped, and it's a cool, pleasant evening in downtown St. Andrews. The traffic on Beck is light, and there's only a few people on the sidewalks and waiting out in front of the bright-yellow building of Hunt's Oyster Bar.

Still, Clyde is wary, always watching, always aware.

"Sorry to disturb you when you with her," he says.

"All good," I say. "What's up?"

"You hear about Lev Sokolov?" he asks.

I nod.

Lev Sokolov, a Russian mobster or a Russian with mob ties, owned the club where Ashlynn works and where I had a run-in with his demented nephew Dimitri.

"Keep expecting Dimitri to make a run at me," I say.

"Probably will eventually," he says, "but he's pretty busy at the moment."

"Shaking down Cloud Nine customers?"

"Trying to survive. Whoever took Lev out may do the same to Dimitri."

"If it wasn't Dimitri," I say.

He nods. "If it wasn't him."

Closing a case is never clean. Even when we get a good result there are always loose ends, always unresolved issues that follow us into the next case. The same is true of life. Rarely do things get wrapped up. So even though Blade and I are embarking on a new case—attempting to find Brooklyn Hill—we're still having to deal with Dimitri and Logan and the fallout from Blade's involvement in Chrissy Violet's disappearance.

"Just wanted you to know I'll be keeping an eye on things," he says. "Do what I can to help—'specially protect that sweet little girl."

I nod. "I appreciate that."

We fall silent a moment, and I glance over at Alana looking at the pictures and pretending to read a picture book about dinosaurs.

The pale, pinkish bricks of the Publishing Museum building, which was built in 1920, look washed out, its many patches and visible repairs resembling a gingerbread house.

The home of several of Panama City's first newspapers, this publishing plant was built by George Mortimer and Lillian Carlisle West. George was a writer, horticulturist, publisher, railroader, attorney, photographer, and entrepreneur, and is considered by many to be the founding father of Panama City. Lillian, his third wife, ran the business, which included commercial printing, following his death and later became the first woman registered to vote in St. Andrews.

Today the building houses personal and business artifacts of the Wests, antique printing equipment, historical exhibits, and serves as a visitor center and the starting point of the St. Andrews historic guided walking tour.

"How is Destiny?" I ask. "She still safe?"

Destiny is a dancer at Cloud Nine and Logan's sometime girlfriend experience. Since Logan got video footage that would send me back to prison, he has been blackmailing me to do certain jobs for him. One of them was to find out if Destiny was cheating on him—something she essentially did with me the first time I met her. She's the reason I got into it with Dimitri, and since then Clyde and I have been keeping an eye on her to make sure she doesn't become one of Logan or Dimitri's victims.

"For now," he says. "Best I can tell things are coolin' off between her and Logan."

"Best thing that could happen to her," I say, though I know she'll only find another loser like Logan to treat her the way she thinks she deserves.

"As long as he the one doin' the coolin'," he says.

"Is he?"

"Think so."

"Good. Really like to get her and Ashlynn out of there."

"Would solve some problems," he says. "And create some others."

"Just one other," I say. "A big ass financial one."

"Get Mommy out of where?" Alana says, looking up from her book.

We're speaking low and I'm surprised she heard me.

"Just get her a different job," I say. "So she could get more nights with you."

The truth is with a different job she'd probably see less of Alana, but she'd be safer.

"Nowhere else they can make bank like that," he says.

"I'd appreciate if you'd keep an eye on Ashlynn too," I say. "Let me know if you hear anything."

"Already on it," he says.

"Thank you."

"And tell Blade I said hit me up she need anything . . . in connection with that crazy chick goin' missin'."

8

"I remember when that happened," Lexi is saying. "Such an intriguing case. It's cool you get to work it."

I nod.

Lexi Miller, a petite, athletic bottle blond with Gulf-green eyes and the body of a runner, might be my girlfriend if she weren't my probation officer. It's against all the rules for us to see each other socially, and she'd lose her job if the wrong people find out.

"But a lot of pressure too," she adds. "Very tough case. Nobody's been able to make any headway on it, have they?"

We are in my tiny kitchen, which is in the corner of my small apartment. It's late. Alana is asleep in my bed, the door slightly ajar so we can see and hear her. We're making chocolate chip cookies. Well, mostly she's making them and I'm assisting.

Alexa is shuffling songs by Amanda Shires so softly we're only catching the occasional phrase and refrain, but barely audible Amanda Shires is better than no Amanda Shires at all.

When I got arrested for aggravated battery on Logan Owens after I found him with a very young girl, the judge took one look at my history of violence and sentenced me to a year and a day of state prison time and two years of probation. I've done my year of state time and now I'm doing my two years of probation, which carried with it many conditions—counseling, anger management support groups, staying away from criminals, not having any weapons, and not so much as a heated argument with anyone. If I violate any of those conditions I'll be sent back to prison and serve out the remainder of my two years, which at this point is nearly all of it. It's Lexi's job to make sure I'm meeting all the conditions of my probation—not helping me violate them.

"Seems like for a while everyone was saying she did a runner and then later that the boyfriend did it, but . . . then they never could figure out how or what even happened, so . . ."

"That about sums it up," I say.

"I vote for jealous bridesmaid," she says with a smile. "And I'm only half kidding. Those bitches be crazy."

"You ever been one?"

"A crazy bitch?" she says. "You know I have."

Not long ago she had shown up on my door with an armed tough guy because she thought I was about to blackmail her—when what really happened was Logan, who had been spying on me, had taken pictures of us together and sent them to her.

"A bridesmaid," I say.

She nods. "I'm embarrassed to say I have."

"Ever done a bachelorette weekend?"

"I'm mortified to say I have. They are absolutely insane—a group of young girls loose on the town with estrogen levels so high it's a wonder there's not spontaneous lactation, drinking their skinny-ass weight in booze and each trying to outdo the other. I know they say Brooklyn Hill's disappearance is an impossible crime, but . . . I'm tellin' you . . . anything's possible at bachelorette parties."

"I'll keep that in mind. First we have to figure out what

happened and how, then we'll get to the who. Think the DA's making a big mistake doing it the other way 'round."

"I agree, but how do you figure out what and how when they're impossible?"

"Wish I knew."

She finishes scooping out the small blobs of cookie dough onto the cookie sheet, puts on an oven mitt, opens the oven door, removes the first batch of cookies, places them on the stovetop, places the second batch in, closes the oven door, removes the oven mitt, and drops it on the counter.

The smell of the freshly baked cookies is so strong I wonder if it might wake up Alana. Inside the warmth of the comforting aroma is a rich, sweet scent with hints of musky earthiness.

There's a tranquil domesticity in our evenings together with Alana, something akin to the comfortableness of homemade chocolate chip cookies.

"I don't think she just ran away," I say. "That's always a popular theory in cases like this. It's the hopeful, happy ending —someone just decided to go get a new life, start over, leave everything and everyone behind. Don't think for one second that wasn't what I hoped for Kaylee. But it's nearly impossible from a psychological standpoint—and unless the person is a very, very wealthy person with enormous liquidity and resources it's impossible from a practical standpoint."

"How do you mean?"

"We're social creatures," I say. "Think about the type of person it would take to leave everyone behind forever—not ever contact them again."

"A sociopath maybe," she says.

"It's hard to imagine anyone who was very connected to people in the first place being able to suddenly and irrevocably disconnect from all of them forever."

"True."

"And then there's the resources it would require," I say.

"You'd have to have an enormous amount of cash, but not just that. You'd have to have fake IDs, documents, credit cards. If not, you couldn't buy or rent a car, stay in a hotel, buy a home or rent an apartment, get a phone, a job. Who could even know where to begin to get those things—even if you had a ton of money hidden away somewhere under some other name. Think about it—if you left your life, you'd have to drop everything. Your phone, your wallet, your car, your bank accounts, your credit cards. If you used any of those things you'd be tracked instantly. When Kaylee and Brooklyn disappeared they never accessed any of their accounts, they never used their phones again, never again logged into social media or anything."

"So probably not a runaway bride," she says.

"Probably not," I say. "Not to mention—why runaway from such a public place with so many people and surveillance cameras around? Why not just vanish from your apartment?"

"Good point."

"But that also works against it being one of her friends or her boyfriend or even a stranger," I say. "There's just not enough time for someone to kill her and hide her or sneak her out. Not nearly enough time. Not to mention there was no sign of her, no evidence, no body, no nothing."

She opens the drawer next to the oven and withdraws a spatula and uses it to remove the cookies from the cookie sheet and place them on a plate.

"I should've asked sooner," she says, "but please tell me you have milk."

"I have milk," I say. "It's one of the few things I always have —so I can make Alana's chokee milk."

"Ah."

I open the upper cabinet, withdraw two glasses, and fill them with milk.

We take the glasses of milk and the plate of cookies over to the table, sit next to each other, and begin to eat.

I break apart one of the soft, warm cookies and watch the steam rise from the gooey center before popping one of the halves into my mouth.

"These are delicious," I say. "Thank you so much for making them."

"Think you'll ever get married?" she asks.

I shrug, taking a moment to finish chewing and drinking another sip of milk before responding. "Haven't given it much thought. You?"

"I don't know. Part of me wants to. Part of me wants nothing to do with it."

I nod. "Guess I've always thought it wasn't for me—so much so I haven't ever thought about it much. I'm talking about on a subconscious level. I don't know, the idea of family is pretty foreign to me."

"The traditional idea, sure," she says. "But you have a family. Blade. Ashlynn. Alana. And others—maybe Ben and Pete and . . ."

"Kaylee," I say. "You're right. That's my family. I'm not sure I'll ever have any other kind. I see some orphans obsessively trying to get and keep what they never had growing up and others . . . never even attempting it. With me . . . I feel like I'm having to rebuild my entire life after getting out of prison and with the threat of it still hanging over me . . ."

"Yeah, I get that. In many ways marriage seems so . . . outdated. Not sure I see the point. But . . . I don't think I'd want to be in a relationship that absolutely ruled it out or definitely had it as the end goal."

I nod and eat another cookie.

"Speaking of relationships," she says. "Any desire to talk about ours?"

"Happy to," I say. "Anything in particular or . . ."

"Just sort of state of the union."

"Okay."

"Are we even *in* a relationship?" she says. "I mean obviously we *relate*, but . . . we've never defined or even really discussed anything—but the obvious."

"That it's illegal and—"

"Not illegal exactly," she says. "At least not for you. I'd lose my job, but I don't think I'd be prosecuted, but I know what you mean."

"Given all that . . . I guess I never thought we could be in a relationship—at least not a real one. And that's before you showed up at my door with muscle because you thought I could be capable of blackmail or extortion or whatever."

"Not my finest moment," she says, "but that was quite a while ago, and I thought we had moved past it."

"We have."

"You said you understood why I thought what I thought and did what I did."

"I do."

"I guess we don't have to be in a certain kind of relationship as long we both know what we're in or not in and have the same expectations."

"Sounds reasonable," I say. "I have no expectations of you. You're taking a huge risk even the little we see each other, so if you ever decide to stop I'd understand. Actually, I do have an expectation now that I think of it. I guess I keep expecting that to happen—you to conclude the risk is just too great and stop coming around."

"I don't see that happening but can see why you would."

She hops up, takes the other cookies out of the oven, and sits back down at the table.

"You're right that that doesn't sound like much of a relationship. Are we exclusive? Are you seeing other people?"

I think about sleeping with Heather Harrison, the mother of the missing girl from our last case.

It was just the once and it was more therapeutic than erotic, and I have yet to tell her about it.

"No," I say.

"To which?"

"Either. If you're dating other people I wouldn't be surprised or bothered."

"Oh," she says, and something changes. "I guess I thought we were exclusive. I'm not dating anyone and I'd feel the need to tell you if I ever decided to."

I nod.

"Are you dating other people?" she asks.

"No."

"Would you tell me if you decided to?"

"Would you want me to?"

She nods. "I would."

"Then I will."

"This didn't go the way I thought it would," she says. "I'm . . . I feel sad. I'm not sure I want to be in a non-relationship relationship with you. Not sure I *can* be."

9

"I remember Brook being upset at the beginning of the night," Zoey says. "Remember? She was on the phone a while before we left and when she got off she was different. She tried to pretend not to be, but I could tell. She got better later but she was never the same."

It's the next evening and Blade and I are in the party bus with four of Brook's bridesmaids—Zoey Wanamaker, Harper Leigh Gallagher, Olivia Lunken, and Willow Rose.

We are retracing the route that these young ladies took with Brook the night of her disappearance and discussing the details they recall along the way.

Zoey Wanamaker, the heaviest of them, is a kindergarten teacher with brown hair and eyes and often speaks like she's talking to children. Harper Leigh Gallagher, an artist with a husband-financed gallery, has dark hair and bright blue eyes, and pale, flawless skin on a round face. Olivia Lunken, a law student and paralegal, is an African-American woman with light caramel skin, straightish shoulder-length black hair and a soft sexy way of speaking. Willow Rose, a yoga instructor and doula, has long, straight auburn hair and a reddish tint to her pale, freckle-flecked skin.

They are all in their early to mid twenties.

Missing from the group are Poppy Paterson, a singer-actress-waitress, and Annabeth Dunn, Liam's sister.

"Emotions were running high," Harper says. "For all of us. It was a stressful time. I remember her being kinda overwhelmed and high strung, but I didn't think she was upset like in a bad way. What'd the rest of y'all think?"

"She was definitely upset after that call," Olivia says. "You think it had something to do with her disappearance?"

"I guess I missed something," Harper says, "but it was a long time before she went missing, and she seemed fine throughout the night, didn't she?"

"Yeah," Zoey says. "She did. She never seemed exactly the same but she got a lot better, so it's hard to see it having anything to do with whatever happened to her."

"Anyone know who she was talking to or what it was about?" I ask. "What she was upset about."

No one does.

Willow says, "I'm sure the police have her phone records. Shouldn't be hard to figure out who she was talking to."

I nod. "True."

"Harper's right though," Willow adds. "We were all emotional that night. It was a wild rollercoaster ride—plus all the drinking and getting overwhelmed and then later worn out by it all. It was all a lot. And it had to be the most difficult on poor Brook."

"That's true," Harper says. "I was exhausted by the end of the night. Totally spent."

"Yeah, I don't think you said a single word on the way back to the hotel," Zoey says.

"I was wiped out. I think I fell asleep and I'm pretty sure I wasn't the only one."

"I was too worried about Brook to sleep," Olivia says.

Blade remains silent, studying the group of young women like they are a new-to-her species.

"Don't think I was worried by that point yet," Zoey says. "Figured we'd find her at the hotel waiting for us or she'd show up later with a big smile on her face because she had just hooked up with Liam. She was like that, would do stuff like that."

Beneath her sweetsy-talking-to-children tone is a layer of disapproval and judgment.

We cross over the Hathaway Bridge and turn off of 98 onto Thomas Drive on our way to Capt. Anderson's.

"I should say that this isn't the vehicle we were in that night," Harper says.

We are in a modified Ford F-550 22-passenger bus. Equipped with a light and sound system, special perimeter seating, a bar, and a stripper pole, it feels like a moving night club.

"This is the one I booked, but they upgraded us to a very posh Hummer limo," Harper says. "It was the first of many upgrades and cool things that happened that night that made it feel magical."

The others express their agreement with this assessment.

We pull into the parking lot of Capt. Anderson's and pull up next to the eighteen-foot, solid-bronze propeller from the English Tanker HMS Empire Mica that is displayed out front.

The Empire Mica was an English tanker that was sunk by a German U-Boat around midnight on June 29, 1942 during World War II. The two torpedoes fired from the U-Boat caused a series of explosions and the loss of thirty-three lives. The Mica floated on a sea of fire and was adrift as it burned for over a day, eventually sinking in over one hundred feet of water south of Cape San Blas.

Owned and operated by the Patronis family since 1967, Capt.

Anderson's is a waterfront seafood restaurant specializing in classic Gulf Coast entrees where if you dine early enough you can watch the fishing fleets unload their catch. With its 725 seats, this Panama City Beach staple serves over 250,000 guests during its eight-month season and is regularly named among America's top-fifty restaurants.

"We came here first for cocktails and dinner," Harper says. "Nothing really eventful happened—unless I'm forgetting something."

The others indicate she isn't forgetting anything.

"Everyone was so nice and accommodating," Harper says. "Our waiter was wonderful—so sweet and attentive to Brook."

"*Wait*," Olivia says. "I just remembered something. I didn't think anything of it at the time and then I guess I just forgot with all the trauma and everything, but our waiter. I'm pretty sure I saw him at Jungle Jim's later that night."

"Are you sure?" Zoey asks. "Why didn't you say anything?"

"Not positive and I want to make it clear I'm not accusing anyone of anything, but I'm reasonably certain he was there. Not the first time we went but the last time."

"When Brook went missing," Harper says.

"Anyone remember his name?" I ask.

"Wasn't it Hudson or something like that?" Zoey says.

"It *was*," Harper says. "No idea what his last name was. But if he showed up at the club later that night . . ."

"We need to have a little chat with him," Blade says.

They are her first words of the night, and everyone stops and stares at her for an awkward moment.

10

———————

"**I**s the driver tonight the same one you had that night?" I ask.

Harper shakes her head. "His name was John or Todd or something like that. He was great. Didn't just drive us places but got us in and out safely."

"Well," Blade says, "except for the bride."

"I guess that's true. I didn't even really think of that. And I don't mean he came in and got us, but every time I texted him we were ready to go he had the limo up front and he was waiting for us at the exit and escorted us to the car."

"He wasn't like a bodyguard or anything," Olivia says. "But he did more than was required."

"He was a real gentleman," Zoey says. "No flirting. No lingering eyes. And though he was most attentive to Brook as the bride, as he should've been, he was very nice to all of us."

"Sounds dreamy," Blade says. "But we'll still have a little talk with him."

"Just let him know we said nothing but good things about him," Zoey says.

"We'll tell him y'all are his biggest fans."

The next stop is farther down Thomas Drive, past the curve and not far from Adam's Even, the sex shop where the now-missing Chrissy Violet worked. It's called Double D's Saloon and has a country and western vibe I would't have thought suited this group of women.

"We didn't stay here long," Harper says. "Not our kind of place. Not sure why it was on our list of stops, but Brook insisted. Everyone pretty much ignored us except for one older bartender. He was nice at first. Gave Brook free drinks but then kept asking for her number and telling her he would show us the best spots when he got off."

"He was a creep," Olivia says.

"Remember his name?" I ask.

No one does.

"Next we went to Splash," Harper says.

We continue down Thomas Drive to the area's only gay bar since the Fiesta in town closed.

"This was the best stop of the night," Harper says. "Everyone was wonderful. We were treated like royalty. No problems with anyone or anything."

"Didn't pay for a single drink here," Willow says.

"Let's hear it for the gays," Blade says.

"I really thought if we went back to any place at the end of the night it'd be here," Zoey says, "but Brook wanted to go back to Jungle Jim's."

We pull out of Splash back onto Thomas and drive up past Ms. Newby's, the now-closed super clubs, and Flamingo South where the Harrisons were living when Leah went missing, and I wonder if Heather is up there right now on the balcony reading or writing poetry. To my surprise I feel a longing inside to be back up there with her, a type of bittersweet nostalgia for the sad time we shared while I was searching for her daughter.

"Too bad Spinnaker and Le Vela are closed," Willow says. "They would've been fun that night."

"Not sure why we passed Ms. Newby's only to come back to it later," Harper says, "but we did."

We take a left on Front Beach and drive to Jungle Jim's.

"So our first time here was fantastic," Harper says. "We had no problems whatsoever. Everyone was great. Harley, our hostess, was a sweetheart and even Chase was—"

"Y'all saw Chase?" I ask.

"Yeah," she says. "He came down and congratulated Brook—even offered us an exclusive private party room up next to his office. Something Harley says he almost never does. But we wanted to be down in the club where the action was."

"Tol' us he stayed in his office all night and never saw y'all," Blade says.

"Then he's lying," Olivia says.

"Came to that same conclusion myself," Blade says.

"We'll talk to him again," I say.

"But we didn't see him the second time we came," Harper says. "And that's when Brook went missing."

"Just 'cause y'all didn't see him don't mean she didn't," Blade says. She then looks at Olivia, "Ain't that right, Perry Mason?"

Olivia smiles and nods.

"From here we went back to Ms. Newby's," Harper says. "Not back in the sense that we had been there before—just that we passed it on our way out here."

We head back east on Front Beach toward Newby's.

"How drunk were y'all by this point?" I ask.

"Definitely had a good buzz going," Harper says. "We were loose and giggly, but no one was falling down or slurring their words, were they?"

"No," Olivia says. "I didn't drink much at all that night. Thought someone should have their wits about them. Everybody was still good. Silly as hell, but still upright."

"What about Brook's demeanor?" I ask.

"To be honest," Olivia says, "she was . . . she seemed more melancholic than I would've expected. Not . . . Maybe that's too strong a word. She didn't seem down exactly, just . . . not as up as I expected her to be. May have nothing to do with her disappearance—probably didn't—but she seemed like she didn't feel like partying. It was like she really enjoyed being with all of us —and I could be projecting here—probably am after what happened, but it was almost like she somehow knew this was going to be our last time together. I don't know. With the party stuff at the clubs and all it was like she was going through the motions, but back here in the limo she was sort of cuddly and circumspect."

Zoey says, "I get what you're saying, but I just thought she was realizing her single days were coming to a close. Maybe even second guessing what she was about to do."

"She could've been," Olivia says. "Probably was. Just tellin' y'all my observations."

"Your sober observations," Harper says, "which have to carry more weight than our drunk ones."

"How was it at Ms. Newby's?" I ask as we pull up.

"Fun," Zoey says.

"Best DJ of the night," Willow says.

"The only bit of weirdness was there was a bachelor party here and they kept trying to get us to join them," Harper says.

"That's right," Zoey says. "I had forgotten about that."

Olivia says, "It was like they wanted to pair up and party together for the rest of the night."

"We politely declined several times," Harper says, "but they were relentless."

"Eventually," Olivia says, "I had to get stern with them."

"Perry Mason had to get stern," Blade says. "I'd like to have seen that."

"You're gonna see it you keep callin' me Perry Mason," she says.

"My bad," Blade says. "Meant no offense. Don't drop a restraining order or anything on me."

"Eventually," Harper says, "we just left."

"Y'all left earlier than you would have because of the bachelor party?" I ask.

She nods.

"Did you see them again that night?" I ask.

She shakes her head. "I don't—"

"Not as a party," Willow says, "but I would've sworn I saw a few of them individually at Jungle Jim's when we went back."

"Get any of their names?" I ask.

Olivia says, "The groom-to-be's name was Steph. Steph . . . Brownell or something like that."

Willow says, "The guy that kept hitting on me was Roland, and he's one of the ones I thought I saw at Jungle Jim's later that night."

"Anything else happen here?" I ask.

They all shake their heads.

Harper says, "Next we drove to a public access point on Front Beach, kicked off our shoes, walked on the sand, put our toes in the water, and had a champagne toast and sweet roast."

"What's that?" Blade asks.

"Instead of saying mean or cutting things," Willow says, "you say kind and affirming things about the person being roasted."

"It was very sweet," Zoey says. "Probably my favorite part of the night."

"Mine too," Willow says.

"Yeah," Harper says, "it was very special—even before what happened. After that we went back to Splash for the drag show, which was great. More than one of the performers brought Brook up and included her in their performances. Then we went back to Jungle Jim's."

"Who's idea was that?" I ask.

"Not sure exactly," Harper says, "but it was Brook's decision. We only did what she wanted to do—all night."

"Okay," I say, "let's go back there and do a walkthrough and see what y'all recall."

"Not looking forward to this," Zoey says. "It's the one part of that night I never want to relive."

11

———

Harley Chandler is waiting for us at Jungle Jim's, which doesn't open for another hour or so.

She hugs Brook's bridesmaids like they're old friends.

"Y'all have the run of the place," she says. "Do what you need to do. I just hope it helps find her."

"Thank you."

"I'll be around if y'all need me," she says. "Just holla."

She holds the door open for us but stays outside and takes a call after we go in.

"I have so much anxiety right now," Zoey says as we ride the escalator up toward the club. "It's my first time back."

"Any of you been back since that night?" I ask.

"I was here the very next morning looking for her," Harper says.

"I've avoided it," Olivia says.

"Me too," Willow adds.

"It's just so hard to fathom how it could've happened," Harper says, glancing up at the security cameras. "There were so many bouncers that night. And there was a cop standing at the top of the landing between the escalator and the door. Remember?"

They do.

"There were two cops out here by the time we left," Olivia says.

"That's right," Zoey says. "There were."

"It seemed so safe," Harper says. "Never crossed my mind that anything could happen to any of us. I didn't freak out until much later."

"None of us did," Zoey says. "Not really."

"Take us through that night," I say. "Tell us everything you remember. You all rode the escalator up together?"

They all nod.

"We did," Harper says.

We step off the escalator, cross the landing, and enter the club.

"What'd y'all do when you came inside?"

"Looked around for a VIP table," Harper says, "but they were all taken."

"The place was really packed at that point," Olivia says.

"I was hoping we'd just turn around and leave," Zoey says, "but Brook wanted to stay."

"We all sort of drifted over to the bar together," Harper says. "When we ordered our drinks, an older man sitting alone at the bar told the bartender to put them on his tab. When we thanked him he told Brook congratulations and that was it. He didn't bother us or anything. Then we looked for any empty tables out here—these little ones out in the middle of the floor. We found a few but not together, so we had to split up."

"I remember it was so loud we couldn't hear each other," Olivia says.

"Take us to the tables y'all sat at," I say. "Who sat together?"

Harper says, "Brook and I were over here."

She walks over to a small hightop cocktail table and takes a seat on one of the stools.

Zoey says, "I was over here with Annabeth—Liam's sister."

She steps over and takes a seat about fifteen feet away from where Harper is seated.

Olivia says, "I was over here with Poppy."

She walks over and takes a seat at a table much closer to the stage and dance floor than the others.

"And I sort of floated between them," Willow says. "Just stood at each table for a while. I started with—actually, I went to the bathroom first, so just sat my drink down on Harper and Brook's table since it was the closest. When I came out I stood at their table for a few then when they went to dance, I moved over to Zoey's and stood there a while."

Harper says, "You didn't stay with our drinks while we were gone?"

"No," Willow says, shaking her head. "I didn't know I was supposed to."

"Do you think someone put something in your drinks?" I ask.

"You did get quiet and out of it," Olivia says. "And slept all the way back to the hotel then crashed when we got there."

"I'm so sorry," Willow says. "I wish I had known. If you asked me to I didn't hear you. It was so loud. I guess I figured you were getting new drinks when you finished dancing. I feel like I'm going to be sick."

"We don't know that anyone put anything in our drinks," Harper says, "or if it had anything to do with Brook's disappearance. And even if it did it's not your fault."

"Did Brook seem out of it or start acting differently at any point?" I ask.

"She seemed tired to me," Harper says, "and tipsy, but I never thought she was anything else."

Olivia says, "I thought she was acting differently all night, so . . ."

"Y'all both drink from your drinks when you came back to your table?" Blade asks.

Harper looks up, squints, twists her lips, then starts nodding slowly. "I believe we did."

"Even though Willow wasn't at your table when you got back?"

"That's the thing," Harper says. "She was."

"Yeah," Willow says, frowning and nodding. "I think by the time they got back I was back over there. It's funny . . . I didn't even think about their drinks, but at a certain point I thought someone might take their table—plus I wanted to sit down—so I went back over."

"No matter how it happened or what exactly happened," Harper says, "it's not your fault. You couldn't hear anything. No one could."

"What else happened?" I ask. "What else did y'all do?"

"A few guys came by and brought Brook drinks and tried to talk to her, but . . . She was polite but didn't really interact with them much."

"Most of us were too tired to do anything," Olivia says. "We all just sort of sat at our tables until . . ."

"Until what?" I ask.

"The last dance of the night," she says. "We all got on the floor for that."

Harper says, "The DJ started doing that thing DJ's do at the end of the night—warning us it was almost closing time. There was a last call for alcohol. Then he was like 'Only two more songs.' Brook and I went to pee so we wouldn't have to on the drive back to the hotel. She finished and came out before I did. When I came out everyone was on the dance floor for the final dance. I thought she was out there too. And she may have been. I just don't know. After the last dance we all sort of met up, but she never joined us. We looked around. Called her phone. Checked the bathroom again. Eventually, we were the only ones left in the place. The staff helped us look around, but she wasn't here, so we figured she was already in the limo, but when we got there she wasn't there either. We looked around outside. By this time the parking lot was empty. She was just gone. We texted her about a hundred times. Told her we'd see her back at the room—figured she was already there. Or with Liam."

"Did you call or text him?" I ask.

"Eventually his sister did," Olivia says. "She was the only one with his number. He never responded until the next morning. Must have been asleep."

"We intended to look for her more, but we all sort of passed out when we got back to the room. When I woke up early the next morning and she still wasn't there and hadn't responded to our texts and messages, I freaked. Went back to the club and started searching for her. But she wasn't there. She wasn't anywhere. And we've never seen her again."

12

———

"Whatta you think?" I ask Blade.

We are driving back to our office after leaving the bridesmaids.

"Even if she was drugged," she says, "still don't know what happened to her or how it was done."

"True," I say. "But it could give us a direction to go in. Wonder if Chase's office and private room were searched."

"Bet they weren't—least not until the next day or even later."

"But we keep running up against the same problem," I say. "Even if he drugged her and got her up to his office somehow the cameras would've caught him taking her out."

"'Less he got a secret room up there he's keepin' her in."

I nod. "Definitely worth checking."

"How?" she says. "Can't exactly break in without being filmed."

"That may be the real reason he has all the bouncers and surveillance cameras. Hell, they could be the ones who bring him the girls."

"It'll be easy if they are," she says. "We can certainly break one of them."

"Wonder how much of the surveillance footage they actually looked at—like how far into the future did they go and how certain they are it hasn't been altered."

"Guy like Chase," she says, "could easily alter the footage— or if this is something he does a lot . . . he could have a secret exit that's not covered by cameras at all."

"We gotta get a better look at that building," I say. "And take a closer look at Chase."

"Yes, we do."

"We also need to meet with the other two bridesmaids who weren't there tonight," I say.

"Yeah. Didn't mention them a lot, did they?"

"No, they didn't."

"Be interesting to get their take on things."

"Also need to track down the old bartender, the bachelor party guys, the limo driver, the waiter from Capt. Anderson's, and the man himself."

"Liam?" I say. "Strange he didn't answer his phone or respond to any of the texts that night."

"Almost like he was busy doing something else," she says.

13

That night I play a solo acoustic gig at the Lie'Brary on Beck.

Alana is with her mother, who is off tonight, Blade is with Rush at her gig at Tootsie's, and Lexi is working late checking in on probationers at their homes. All of which means I have a rare night alone—something I enjoy and don't get enough of.

There's a small crowd during my first set—a few couples having a quiet drink in the back, a few single guys sitting at the bar drinking beer and talking to the young female bartender.

Before beginning to play all I wanted to do was follow up on some of the leads we uncovered with the bridesmaids this afternoon, but once I start playing everything else fades into the deep background—all my cares and concerns, worries and stresses, the threats hanging over me. Everything recedes, the music becoming a small sailboat on a tranquil sea.

Instead of thinking about how we probably won't solve Brook's case or how likely it is I or Blade or both of us will be going to prison soon or how Logan or Dimitri could sneak up behind me and back-shoot me at any moment, I concentrate on my new mashup, my own arrangement of *I Can See Clearly* and *Here Comes the Sun*. Instead of worrying about Ashlynn and Alana and Destiny I combine *Drift Away* and *Listen to the Music* and drift away on a lazy flowing river that frees my soul. And instead of being overwhelmed by the flood of fascism and the rise of right-wing militias fueled by racism, sexism, and crazy conspiracy theories and the aggressions and atrocities of autocratic regimes around the world I focus on playing and singing *Imagine.* Even though I'm no longer able to imagine such a world. If I ever was.

Halfway through my second set, Heather Harrison walks in, and I'm happy to see her.

She brings her large glass of red wine and sits at a small table right in front of where I'm playing.

Cutting my second set a little short, I take a break and join her at the table.

"How are you?" I ask. "It's so good to see you."

"I'm okay," she says. "Better thanks to you and your partner. How are you?"

I shrug. "I'm . . . okay. Better now. I actually thought about you today. A case we're working on took me by Flamingo South, and I wondered if you were up there on the balcony."

She smiles. "Don't spend as much time there these days."

"That's what I figured," I say. "What are you doing with your days these days?"

"More than I used to," she says. "Thanks to you. Writing more—and not just about Leah. Living a little."

"That's good."

"Malcolm and I split up," she says.

I had found out what happened to her daughter, but that hadn't solved all her problems.

"We'd been hanging by a thread for . . . well even before Leah went missing," she says. "Only stayed together because she was missing. Once we . . . knew . . . we had no reason to . . . And . . . I just couldn't forgive him for what he did."

I nod slowly. "I certainly understand."

"I know you need to get back to playing," she says. "Think we could go somewhere and talk afterward."

"Sure," I say.

I play my final set, then she helps me tear down and load out, then we walk around St. Andrews for a while, eventually winding up in Oaks by the Bay.

The park is quiet and empty, and we make our way down the boardwalk to the deck by the water.

It's dark, and the lights of the buildings on the other side of the bay look like a coastal town seen from out at sea. The moon and stars and the various lights reflect off of the undulating surface of the water and shimmer serenely.

"This is so nice," she says. "Thank you."

"I love it here."

"I'm not entirely sure why I came tonight," she says.

"I'm glad you did."

"It was partly to say *thank you* again," she says. "You gave me my daughter and my life back. I can never thank you enough, but I have to keep tryin'. But it was also because I was hoping for this—to get some time alone with you. In all this time . . . you were—*are*—the only person I feel completely comfortable around. I . . . I know I'm not . . . this isn't coming out exactly right, but what I mean is . . . I feel the most like myself when I'm with you."

"That may be the single greatest compliment I've ever received," I say.

"There's no one else I can tell that I feel free in a way that I haven't since the moment Leah went missing. Or that for the first time since then I want an actual life. And how guilty I feel about that—*sometimes*. And only sometimes."

I take her hand in mine and place my other hand above it.

"I feel . . . the emotion—I'm not even sure it *is* an emotion—that I'm experiencing the most is relief. I feel such a sense of relief to know what happened to her and where she is . . . And sometimes I feel like . . . like the largest part of my grief was the not knowing and now that I know I'm . . . starting to feel . . . more . . . okay, more normal. But that makes me think I'm a horrible mother, a sociopath of a person. Was I really plagued more by the intellectual anguish of not knowing what happened to her than the emotional hollowing out of the actual loss of her?"

"I'm happy just to listen," I say, "but I'd like to respond to that if you don't mind."

"Please."

"The answer to your question is *no*. Your grief at the loss of Leah is as deep and profound as any I've ever witnessed. But you've been grieving over a decade. You've only known what happened to her for a few weeks. It's new and it's powerful and it's liberating. It may even be taking up all the oxygen in your emotional room right now, but only because it's new. You have suffered the very worst thing a human being can suffer. Nothing else comes close. Take any relief and return to normalcy you are fortunate enough to get. There's no roadmap or instructions for what you're experiencing. There's no one way or right way to navigate it. You're doing . . . amazing. Give yourself a break. Be as kind and gentle with yourself as you are everyone else."

"You're . . . nearly young enough to be my son. How do you know so much . . . How are you so wise?"

"I'm not. I'm nothing. But I know loss. I know grief."

14

———

Later that night I meet with Todd Johns, the limo driver for Brook's bachelorette party.

The long, black Cadillac limo he's driving tonight is parked in the VIP spot in front of Cloud Nine—the strip club where Ashlynn works.

We're standing near the front of it talking, watching as mostly men and a few couples walk into the club.

I wonder if Dimitri is around and if I'll have a confrontation with him before the night is over and I'm glad that Ashlynn isn't working.

"I'm retired military," Todd Johns is saying. "Just looking for something to do."

His closely cropped hair and lean, muscular physique say military, but his youthfulness says anything but retired.

"Put my twenty in and got out. Now I don't know what to do with myself. I tried being a correctional officer, but that wasn't for me. I'm used to discipline, and those are the most undisciplined men on the planet. I'm looking at maybe doing law enforcement, but I'm not sure. The limo thing is my brother-in-law's company. I'm just helping out until I figure out my next move. But I take it seriously and try to do a good job. I try to get all the passengers where they're going and in and out of the places they're going and back home carefully and safely."

I nod.

"Sure enjoy the bachelorette parties more than the bachelor," he says, glancing back at Cloud Nine. "And that was a good group of girls. One of the better ones I've had. Most everyone was polite and had good manners and were nice to each other. The bride was very special. You can tell some people just have that thing. Know what I mean? She could've been a Hollywood actress or something. But she wasn't conceited or anything. Seemed to me to be the kind of pretty girl who doesn't know she's pretty—or at least doesn't dwell on it. I tell you . . . felt bad for her. When I first picked them up she was so happy—giddy even, but then she got a phone call and everything seemed to change. She stepped outside the vehicle to take it and talked for a while. The conversation didn't seem animated or heated or anything, but boy did it put a damper on the rest of the night. She never was the same. The other girls tried to cheer her up, were very sweet to her and she did get better but she was never the same."

"Any idea who she was talkin' to or what it was about?"

He shakes his head. "No idea."

"Group dynamics in situations—'specially like that one are always interesting. Usually you have everyone tripping over themselves to prove they're the bride's best friend, but that distinction was clearly reserved for the young woman who booked the vehicle—Harper something, I think. She was in charge that night. I mean she deferred to Brook and did what she wanted, but she was like the organizer and cheerleader, the facilitator for whatever the bride wanted. It seemed like all of them were pretty close and comfortable with each other 'cept two of them. Don't know their names, but they definitely seem like observers. Not that they minded.

Didn't seem like they did but they were definitely on the outside."

"Anything odd or strange or out of the ordinary happen that night?" I ask.

"Couple of things," he says. "Bachelor party came out of one of the clubs—can't remember which. Think it was Ms. Newby's. Tried to get in the car. Said they wanted to surprise the girls. Said the two groups had decided to spend the rest of the evening together. 'Course I didn't let them. Sent them on their way. When the young women got back in the vehicle they didn't mention anything about it except to say they were leaving early because of how some of the guys were harassing them. My guess was it was the same guys."

I nod.

"When I was parked outside, Splash guy comes up and asks if this is the Brooklyn Hill bachelorette party limo. Told him that was classified information. Lied and told him it wasn't but I wouldn't tell him whose it was. Asked him why he wanted to know before I sent him on his way. Said he was just planning a surprise for her. Didn't realize it at the time, but when I saw a picture of her fiancé later I realized it was him. Liam somebody. I let the detectives on the case know, but I never heard anything else from it."

"Sounds like you were on top of things."

"Don't know what I could've done differently, but I still feel guilty as hell about what happened. I failed to protect her, to get her home safely. I know I wasn't hired as security. Wasn't inside the clubs with them or . . . but I still feel responsible. And I always will. Anything comes up I can do to help you find her, let me know."

"Thanks. I definitely will. Anything else?"

"I know she was already missing by this point, but when I took them back to the hotel I saw a car idling in the parking lot and then I saw her fiancé again but didn't think anything of it at the time. I figured he was supposed to meet up with them after their night out or something. After I got done getting them safely inside the hotel I went and checked out the idling car. I thought at the time I was just being paranoid—and after I saw who was inside I knew I was, but just thought I'd mention it anyway. Give you a full account of the night. There were two older ladies inside an old panel van with no markings on it. One of them looked like somebody's grandma and the other one . . . well, she sort of look like somebody's grand*pa*."

I'm about to say something when Dimitri walks out the front door and over to us.

"Hey, guy," he says. "Vat? You zink you just going to hang here in my parking lot and I not come out and shoot you?"

Dimitri is a lean, muscular man with closely cropped hair in his late twenties or early thirties. He's wearing an expensive black suit with a black silk shirt unbuttoned halfway down his chest.

"Eet ees disrespectful," he says.

He speaks with a heavy Russian accent—replacing *i* with *ee*, randomly omitting the articles *a* and *the,* rolling his *r*'s, harshing his *h*'s, softening his *e*'s, and replacing his *th*'s with *z*'s and his *w*'s with *v*'s.

I look at Todd Johns, who has adopted a defensive stance and is looking on with wary interest. "Zis is Dimitri. Dimitri. He tried to shake me down in the parking lot while I was working my last case. When I wouldn't let him he threatened to shoot my dick off and my partner sliced him up a bit. Now he's carrying a vendetta against me."

"Guy, you got beeg balls to come and stand out here in front my beezness like zis."

"I'm just working," I say. "Interviewing a witness. Didn't intend any disrespect."

"Maybe you hear I have beeger fish to fry right now. Think you are safe. But I weel geet to all fish eventually, even little tadpole like you. Uncle Lev is gone. And with heem your protection. How does it feel to know I am going to keel you?"

"If I'm honest, not great," I say.

"You are safe right here right now. I am not going to do eet in front of my club. You must know zis, guy, and zis is why you come heer like zis. But eet ees deesrespectful and for zis I make you pay extra. Before I keel you I find some people you care about and I hurt zem real bad."

I nod. "That seems like a reasoned response for me talking to someone in your parking lot."

"You funny guy, sure. Laugh now. Because pain is coming."

15

———

"Your client was stalkin' Brook the night she disappeared," Blade says to Ben.

It's the next morning and the three of us are in our office.

"You sure?" Ben says.

"He came up to the limo driver when the bridal party was in Splash and asked him if he was driving for Brook," I say. "And at the end of the night when the driver dropped them off at the hotel he was there."

"Bet he didn't tell you any of that either, did he?" Blade says.

"But if he was at the hotel when they got there he probably didn't have anything to do with Brook's disappearance. She vanished from Jungle Jim's not the hotel."

"Maybe," I say. "Or maybe she was in his trunk at the time."

"So he snatches her from Jungle Jim's—*how* we still don't know—then goes to the hotel to see her bridesmaids?" Ben says.

"Could've been establishing an alibi or seeing what they knew or "

"It's thin, but I'll ask him."

"We'd like to be there when you do," Blade says.

"You're welcome to talk to him, but when *I* do it's going to be under attorney-client privilege, so it'll have to be just the two of us."

"Pete got us a copy of the phone records," I say.

"Yeah?" he says.

"Everyone says Brook got a call early in the evening that changed everything," I say. "Altered her entire demeanor and put a damper on the rest of the night."

"Let me guess," he says. "The call was to my client."

"*From* him, yeah," I say.

"Okay. I'll talk to him about that too. And no matter what his answers are this is all very helpful stuff. Thank y'all. I need to know everything I can in order to defend him."

"If he's guilty," Blade says, "you gonna have to defend him from us."

"I hope you're talkin' about as state's witnesses and not what you did to Chrissy Violet."

"You have no idea what I did to Chrissy Violet," she says. "Or—"

"Why don't you tell us?" Bob Kirkland says as he walks into the office.

Kirk, as he is known to his colleagues, is the Bay County Sheriff's investigator working Chrissy Violet's disappearance.

"I tol' y'all's asses about not closing the door when we talkin'," Blade says.

Kirkland is a shortish, middle-aged white man with a halo of closely cropped light-brown-going-gray hair and a bit of a soft belly. His reddish face looks perpetually sunburned, and he has deep furrows in his forehead and long crow's feet at the corners of his eyes.

"I don't know," he says. "I like the warm welcome of an open door."

He walks in and stands against the wall across from the desk so he can see all three of us.

"Can y'all spare a few minutes for me?"

Ben says, "I've told you to contact me to set up an appointment, but my client has nothing to say."

"It's okay," Blade says. "I'm happy to have a little chat right now."

"Thank you," Kirkland says. "Won't take up much of your time. Been wantin' to talk to you too, Mr. Burke."

I nod and give him a *get on with it* gesture.

"'Cause I believe you were there that night too," he says.

"Where what night?" I ask.

"Safe Self-Storage," he says. "The night Ms. Violet went missing—three weeks ago today. But you knew what I meant. You two are inseparable, partners, a team. Thing is . . . we searched the storage unit and found all the sick shit Ms. Violet had in there. We know she was holding at least two individuals hostage—in what looks like a very humiliating and degrading way. And given the nature of the things we found inside . . . I'd say she was committing sexual assault against those very victims. DA says given that we can plea this thing down to something very reasonable. Everyone understands retaliation —especially in a sick situation like this one. Hell, a jury might see it as self-defense. And it probably was."

"What makes you think we were there?" I ask. "Places like that have security cameras, don't they? What's on them?"

"The perps broke into the office and stole the system, and the place didn't have an offsite backup."

"That sounds far more like theft than anything else," I say. "Were units burglarized that night?"

"Sounds like Ms. Violet's was," Blade says.

"Her vehicle was found there," he says. "That's where she went missing from."

"Unless she was part of the burglary team and just left in the truck with them," I say.

"There is no burglary team," he says. "She didn't break into her own unit and steal some of her stuff."

"Then she must have been in there when the burglars came or came in on them while they were inside and they snatched her."

"Couldn't afford to have a witness," Blade says.

"Wrong place, wrong time," I say. "Explains everything."

"There are no burglars," he says. "What you're saying doesn't explain anything."

"Oh," I say. "Well, just trying to be helpful. But it's hard without knowing all the facts. If you care to share the file we can give you a better guess at a theory."

"A young woman is missing," he says. "Her family is worried sick about her. I know y'all know what that's like. I've heard about your missing foster sister."

He pauses and we wait.

"I . . . have to admit that I was out in the hallway for a little while before coming in," he says. "Overheard a few things."

"Which aren't admissible in a court of law," Ben says.

"Of course," he says. "Not the point. The point is I know y'all work missing persons cases. I know you're working one right now—the poor bride who went missing last year. I heard you tell Ben here that if his client the boyfriend had anything to do with it you'd go after him. How can you sit here and not see the sick, twisted irony of that? The hypocrisy is astounding. You're trying to find a missing woman and whoever took her is not safe from you. But in Chrissy Violet's case that's you. You are the bad guys you're trying to find—just in a different case. Think about that."

"That's enough," Ben says. "What is this?"

"Okay," Kirkland says. "I'll go. But if y'all are really finders of missing persons do the right thing and help me find Chrissy. Or turn in your PI license and go full criminal."

"Tell you what," Blade says. "If you find her and we had something to do with it we'll turn in our PI ticket, but if we find her and we didn't have anything to do with it you turn in your badge."

He shakes his head. "I don't bet with my badge. But my offer still stands. Tell me where she is and you'll get a fair shake from me and a sweet deal from the DA."

16

———————

"He's got a point," I say.

"Yeah? You think so?" Blade says.

We are driving over to the campus of Gulf Coast State College to meet Liam Dunn.

"You don't?" I ask.

She shrugs. "Sure, he got some points. But they may be based on some faulty underlying suppositions."

"What does that mean?"

"Something that's alleged or supposed," she says.

"Cute."

"I meant just what I said. Everybody got opinions and judgements, but they don't know shit."

"Why don't you tell me everything so I can base my opinions and judgments on what really happened?"

"Do I have your support no matter what happened or what I did?"

"You know you do," I say.

"Then knowin' shit won't change shit."

"It won't change that."

"This whole thing a test," she says. "So far you the only one passin'. Ben, maybe, but he's just doin' his job."

"Don't know about that, but . . . what Kirkland said really hit me hard. I'll always back your play no matter what it is, but . . . I'm not sure I can do this type of work if . . . But if I can't I'll quit the work, not you."

"You ever do something without really thinking it through and it turns into something you didn't expect?" she asks.

"All the damn time."

"I'm searching for an offramp but can't find one so far."

"Let me know how I can help."

"Like I said . . . you passin' with flyin' colors. But I knew you would. Wasn't you I was worried about."

I figure she means Rush, but I'm not sure I understand anything she's saying.

We pull into the parking lot in front of the Social Science building where Liam is waiting for us, and I let it go for now.

Liam is in his tan and black uniform standing next to his black and tan patrol car.

The shade from his hat and his sunglasses obscures much of his face and hides his intense blue eyes, and his uniform camouflages some of the softness his street clothes revealed when Ben first introduced us to him.

"I appreciate y'all meetin' me here," he says. "I spoke to one of the classes this morning and now I'm heading to a meeting in Tallahassee so this little window I have here is my only one today."

"We appreciate you fitting us in," I say. "We just have a couple of quick questions for you and we'll let you get to your meeting."

"Fire away," he says.

"We understand you and Brook had a pretty intense phone conversation near the beginning of the bachelorette night. Can you tell us what it was about?"

"Sure," he says. "And it wasn't all that intense. She didn't like what I was saying, but it never got heated or anything."

"Several people said her demeanor changed after that call," I say.

"I'm sure it did and I feel bad for that, but it turns out I was right, so . . ."

"Right about what?" Blade asks.

"Y'all remember those disturbances we had at the beach back then?" he says.

"I worked them. Never seen anything like it."

In what can only be described as planned and orchestrated chaos, young people, mostly from Alabama and Georgia, came down to the beach on the weekends and wreaked havoc. They blocked intersections, trashed stores, fired weapons, terrorized tourists—seemingly with no greater goal in mind.

"I told her it wasn't safe out there and I either wanted her to stay on this side of the bridge or let me follow them in my civilian vehicle to make sure they were safe. That's all it was. I was genuinely worried for her safety—and it turns out I had every reason to be. But she thought I was trying to spy on her or keep her from doing certain things, but I swear to you that wasn't the case. Her reaction was extreme. Never really seen her act like that before. So I backed off. Told her I wouldn't follow them, but to let me know if they ran into any trouble at all and I'd come running. She said I'd ruined her night and she wasn't even looking forward to going, but I explained how I was just worried about her safety and I wasn't trying to keep her from having a good time. By the time we wrapped up the call she was fine. She wasn't as upbeat and excited as she was before it, but she was a lot better."

"So you's just concerned 'bout her safety," Blade says.

"Right. And I was right to be. At the time I wish I had never made the call but now I wish I had insisted on her letting me protect her."

"So you told her you wouldn't follow them that night," I say.

"Right."

"But then you did."

He shakes his head. "No. I didn't. I didn't follow them. One time when she wasn't answering my texts I went out looking for her. But I never went in any of the clubs. I just tried to find them. Asked a few limo drivers if they were driving her. No one would tell me and I realized how futile it was and by that time she had started texting me back, so I went back home."

"That means your friend who says he was with you at your place all night lied for you," I say.

"Well, not exactly. He went with me. So he was with me the entire night and knew I hadn't done anything."

"So you went looking for her and when you heard from her you went back home," I say.

He nods.

"But then you went back out again."

"No. Not that night."

"We have a witness who saw you at the bridal party's hotel at the end of the evening."

"Then they're mistaken," he says. "Wasn't me. I didn't get back out that night. I wish I had, but I was trying to honor her wishes and not have her pissed at me at the wedding. Now I wish she had been. I wouldn't've minded an angry bride and wife. She could've been mad at me for the rest of our lives and it would've been just fine with me."

17

———

"If Liam said it, it's true," Annabeth says.

Annabeth is a tattoo artist at Blackheart Ink, a small boutique parlor on the beach. She's a smallish late-twenties woman with bottle black hair and pale white skin largely covered with black ink. The black and white bandana holding her hair up and the tiny black wife beater she's wearing reveal the intricate artwork that covers the canvas of her skin, including the large, solid black heart on her chest and breasts.

"He's like the most straight edge person I know," she says. "I mean for real. The only way he could do Brook harm is by boring her to death."

Like the artist herself, her shop is black and white with a goth biker babe feel.

Because of her busy schedule and limited time we are forced to speak with her while she works. A large, topless white woman is face down on Annabeth's black table, her huge breasts flattening and pressing out on the sides. The image Annabeth is inking on the entirety of her enormous back is that of a serpent coiled around a naked woman on a cross.

Beneath the incessant buzzing of the ink gun I can make out the agitation-inducing sounds of angry metal music.

"He's like a little soldier," she says. "He always—and I mean *always*—does what's right. He follows the rules. And his mission in life is to protect and serve—especially his family, friends, and loved ones. He would've gladly died for Brook, seen it as his duty, considered it a good death and all that way of the samurai shit."

She stops talking for a moment to concentrate on what she's doing, filling in the red glow of the serpent's eyes, moving the needle back and forth with one black latex-gloved hand while wiping excess ink and blood away with the other.

"You okay, Kong?" she asks the woman lying on the chair. "Need a break?"

Kong lifts her right arm slightly and gives Annabeth a thumbs up signal.

"I've done work for both of you, haven't I?" Annabeth says to us.

We nod.

"Still happy with it?"

We nod again.

"Didn't know I had PIs for clients," she says. "May have to swap out some ink for some investigating some day."

"We'd be down," I say.

"I know what you should do," she says. "Talk to his ex-girl-friends. That way you don't have to take my word for it—or anyone else's. No ex has any reason to lie to you about him. And he doesn't have that many. Won't take you long to run them down. Hell, I can give you the names and numbers of most of them."

"That'd be helpful," I say. "Thanks."

Beneath every word we utter is the constant droning buzz of the tattoo gun and the screaming of the guitars and vocals of the metal music.

I add, "Can you tell us about that night?"

"Wasn't much to it," she says. "Those are some straight edge, boring-ass, kindergarten-teacher type white girls. The only reason I was included—the only reason I'm a bridesmaid—is because I'm the groom's sister. I wanted to say *no* but didn't feel like I could. I've disappointed my family enough. And I sure as shit didn't want to do this lame ass bachelorette night bullshit but . . . didn't feel like I had a choice. So I went. I trailed after them all night, mocking them in my head and drinking enough to make it less like someone was driving a railroad spike into my eye with a sledgehammer."

"Anything happen that looking back may have had something to do with her disappearance?"

She shakes her head. "Just the usual bachelorette bullshit. Unless one of the guys buying her drinks and dancing with her was a psycho killer . . . don't know of anything that portended her disappearance."

"What'd you think of Brook?" Blade asks.

She shrugs. "She's okay, I guess. Slightly less boring than my brother. She was gorgeous and really had a certain . . . charisma. Definitely out of my brother's league. He was a reacher and she was a settler, but I think he made her feel safe and she was happy to take that tradeoff."

"And you don't have any idea what happened to her or who was behind it?"

"None. I barely knew her. I just hate it for my lame ass brother. No way he's gonna get another girl like her. And he knows it."

"He don't seem too broken up about it," Blade says.

"That's just because of his stoic samurai code. He can't show it, but he really is."

I hand her a card. "Thanks for your time. You think of anything, please give us a call."

"Let me get that list for you," she says.

She rips out a corner of a page in a nearby sketch pad and quickly jots down a list of names and numbers and hands it to me.

I glance at it and hold it up to blade and point to the middle name.

"*Oh shiiiit*," Blade exclaims. "Motive much?"

18

——————

"Why didn't you tell us you and Liam used to date?" Blade asks.

Zoey Wanamaker looks up from the old red schoolhouse brick she is painting. "I don't know. I guess it just never came up. I guess I thought y'all knew."

Blade and I are in her empty classroom at the end of the school day just after the students had gone home. She is seated at a low table in a small, low chair, both of which exaggerate her heaviness and give her an unfair elephantine quality.

Her kindergarten classroom is all bright primary colors and pictures of puppy dogs. Miniature desks on a bright blue rug face a bulletin board filled with colorful cartoons of ABCs and 123s. And though it smells of sweaty, sticky little kids and Frito feet, there's the sickly sweet aroma of air fresheners and scented candles attempting to cover it.

"That's a lot of guessin'," Blade says. "And how the hell would we know?"

"I don't know, but don't be mean to me," she says, turning to me. "Don't let her be mean to me."

"Don't be mean to her," I say to Blade.

"Sweetheart," Blade says in softest, most gentle, most insincere voice, "how the heck would we know?"

"From the other girls I guess. I don't know. I wasn't trying to keep it from you. It's not some big secret or anything. I guess I thought everyone knew. I'm the one who introduced them."

Nearly all her words come out slowly and animatedly as if she's speaking condescendingly to small children. Hazards of the job, I guess.

"Why you paintin' a brick?" Blade asks.

The brick she is painting flowers and butterflies on is one of many on the table before her.

"They're from the old Jefferson schoolhouse that was torn down. I'm letting my kids decorate them and then take home a little piece of history."

"That's nice," I say, trying to make up for Blade's meanness.

"So you and Liam were still together when he started seein' Brook?" Blade says.

"Yeah. *No.* Not when they—when they met. They started seein' each other after we broke up."

"I bet you really believe that too," Blade says.

"I do. It's true. Liam would never cheat. He's got a strong moral code he lives by."

"Less sure about Brook?" I ask.

She shrugs. "She's a good friend. I don't think she would do anything like that, but I know Liam never would."

She puts the brick down and steps over and begins returning books to their shelf.

We follow her and are now standing near a bright yellow reading rug with a rocking chair and small bookshelf on the far corner of it. The books are mostly the large picture variety with lots of colorful images and very few words. I notice a couple by Paul McCartney from his Grandude series. Alana has the same ones.

"Why did you go that night?" I ask.

"Why are you in their wedding?" Blade says.

"She's still my friend."

"Frenemy more like it," Blade says. "Why would they want you in their wedding?"

"I'm tellin' you we're all still friends. Brook and I are great friends. I love her. I'm happy for them. I have nothing but respect for Liam. He's truly one of the good ones."

"Be happier if he was still with you though, wouldn't you?" Blade says. "And now he can be."

"It's been a year," she says. "He hasn't so much as glanced my way. Probably all this weight I put on when he broke up with me."

"So your plan didn't work," Blade says.

"My *plan*? My plan to get him back by murdering my close friend? *That plan*? Are you serious? I thought they said you two were good at this. I look like a cold-blooded killer to you?"

"That's what makes it so genius," Blade says.

"Okay," she says, "well, good luck proving it or gettin' anyone to believe it."

19

We find Poppy Paterson in a shed she uses for a music room behind her parents' backyard in Lynn Haven, a suburb of Panama City.

She's a mid-twenties young woman with straight brown hair pulled back into a ponytail that flows out of the back of the cap she's wearing. The baseball-style cap is gray with white lettering on the front that says "Without Music Life Would B ♭ ." She has olive skin, green eyes, and large bright-white teeth. She's somewhat attractive but has eyes that are too close together and a nose that is too large for her face, probably preventing her from getting many of the roles she might otherwise.

Though from the outside the structure we're in looks like all the other wooden storage sheds in all the other yards, the inside looks and feels like a posh Nashville studio.

Plush carpet on the floor, guitars hanging from the walls, which are covered with sound-absorbing acoustic panels, a leather couch seating area in the control room, and a recording booth equipped with a large Neumann mic.

We are in the control room with her—Blade and I on the

couch, Poppy in the office chair at the mixing board. Our shoes, which she asked us to take off before coming in, are on the mat outside the front door.

"Give me just a minute to finish this up," she says.

Playback of one of her original songs pours through the small studio speakers mounted on the wall on either side of the window into the studio.

Her voice is soft and airy and sounds like so many of the popular young singer-songwriter white girls on Youtube these days. Her melody is strong if familiar, her playing is fine, but her lyrics are trite and her rhymes forced and awkward.

After making a few adjustments that produce no discernible difference to the track, she stops playback and swivels her chair around to face us.

"I try to create something every day," she says. "A song. A poem. A monolog. I try to audition for a part in a play or a role in a commercial or TV show and send out a demo to a publisher or artist every week."

"Impressive," I say.

"It's what it takes," she says. "Everything I do is an investment in me as an artist and in my future success. I'm sacrificing now—living with my parents, working shit service jobs—knowing that it will pay off one day. I'm sure you know what I mean. I've seen you play. You're not bad. I like some of your arrangements and mashups. They're different."

"Thanks," I say.

"I've only ever heard you do covers," she says. "Have you written any originals?"

"Working on some," I say. "How did you know Brook?"

"Through creativity," she says. "Before she stopped we were going on a lot of the same auditions, singing in some of the same places. She was . . . one of the most talented people I've ever encountered. She was beautiful too. The camera loved her. I'm always shocked when people like that walk away from it. I guess it's because they take it for granted. They've always had *it* so it doesn't mean as much, maybe. I don't know. I really think she could've been a star, but she quit all of it and never looked back. That was about a year ago. She wouldn't do anything in public, but sometimes I could get her to come over here and play around with me, and I could tell she loved it. Ate it up. And if I'm bein' honest . . . she always blew me away—as in off the stage. All that talent and . . . just decided not to do anything with it—publicly at least. But she'd come over here and show out like Beyoncé."

"What can you tell us about that night?" I ask.

"Not much," she says. "I didn't really participate. I didn't know the other girls, and they weren't really my type, so I mostly just worked on songs in my head most of the night. To tell you the truth . . . I think the only reason she asked me to be a bridesmaid was because she didn't have enough. I don't think she had very many friends, which I could never understand, but . . . I think the only reason she asked me and the groom's sister is so she'd have a bridesmaid for every groomsman he wanted."

"Anything odd or strange happen?" I ask. "Anything that you look back on after she went missing and see differently now?"

She shakes her head. "Sorry. I was in my own little world. Most of the places we went I either went outside or into the bathroom to work on stuff. And I'd go back to the limo way before the others did. So I didn't see or hear much of anything —and nothing sus or anything. I wish I had. I can't believe such a talent is just . . . gone."

20

Brook's bridal party ascends the escalator up to Jungle Jim's like they're starring in a reality TV show. They are stylish, sexy, and stand with attitude. Brook is wearing a large gold pair of sunglasses with white lenses, the word BRIDE written across them in gold script—the B and the R on the left lens, the ID, and E on the right. Each bridesmaid has white sunglasses with white lenses, TEAM written in black on the left lens and BRIDE written in gold on the right.

I'm watching the surveillance footage from the night of Brook's disappearance on my phone as Blade and I ride the escalator up to Jungle Jim's with Harley Chandler.

We are here ostensibly to do another walkthrough while watching the security footage, which we want to do and will find helpful, but our real reason for being back here several hours before the club opens is to get a look at Chase Stevenson's private party room while he's not here.

The footage shows the women entering the club, looking around, making their way over to the bar, getting drinks, and them splitting up among different hightop tables near the dance floor—all exactly like they said.

"Where is the security system kept?" I ask.

"Upstairs next to Chase's office," Harley says.

"May we take a look at it?" I ask.

"Sure," she says. "Anything you like. "

"We need to see everything we didn't last time," I say. "Every room. Every closet. Every nook and cranny."

"You have the run of the place," she says.

"Let's start upstairs," I say.

"This way."

"And we may be joined by the K-9 officer who headed up the search a little later. He's not sure if he can get here in time, but he'll text me if he does."

"Just let me know and I'll let him in."

As we walk up the stairs, I continue to examine the security footage. The place is packed and I lose the bridesmaids from time to time but their actions and movements match their statements—where they sat and who they sat with— Harper and Brook at a table to the right near the restrooms, Zoey and Annabeth across from them on the left side of the room, Olivia and Poppy up close to the stage and dance floor, and Willow floating around between them. Brook and Harper going to dance, Willow standing at their table for a few before leaving it to visit with the other women in the party. Willow returning just before Brook and Harper did.

The footage is too dark and grainy and shot from too far away to see if anyone put something in Brook and Harper's drinks.

We reach the security room and Harley unlocks the door and lets us in.

The room is larger than I expected and has employee lockers and a small break area with a fridge and microwave on one side and the security system on the other. Above a large desk with the security monitor console and computer on it and a leather high back office chair in front of it, mounted monitors display the various camera feeds.

Harley says, "State of the art. Chase spares no expense when it comes to the safety and protection of his patrons."

"It's very impressive," I say. "Where are the blindspots? What's not covered?"

"I think just the restrooms," she says.

"What about Chase's office?" I say. "I don't see a feed from there."

"Oh, yeah. I thought you meant where the customers could go. Chase's office isn't . . . doesn't have cameras."

"How about his private party room?" Blade says.

She hesitates a moment before saying, "He does have a room up here, but it's not a—I've never heard it called a private party room."

"Are there cameras in it?" I ask.

"I don't believe so."

"Can we see it?" Blade asks.

Harley hesitates again. "Ah . . ."

"Full access," Blade says. "Run of the place. Remember?"

"Of course," she says. "I . . . I was just thinking I wish Chase was here. I never go into his office or . . . his . . . room when he's not here."

"Just a quick look," I say. "So we can say we've seen every place here. We won't touch anything."

She nods slowly like it's taking extra effort for her to do so. "Okay," she says. "He did say let you go anywhere you wanted."

She leads us back into the hallway and over to Chase's office, which isn't locked.

When we step into his office the small lights in the ceiling come on slowly. She then leads us over to the back right corner where a hidden door in the wall opens when she lifts a book on the shelf next to it and presses the button beneath it.

The small space beyond the secret door looks like the

champagne room at a posh strip club—mirrored walls and ceilings, a leather loveseat, a table for drinks on either side of it, all of which is dimly lit in moody blues and magentas.

"Do you know if this area was searched the night Brook vanished or the next day?"

"I think everywhere was searched, but I don't know for sure. I can ask Gainer, our head of security. He would know."

"Could you call him in so we could talk to him and the K-9 guy at the same time?"

"I can try."

"There any other rooms up here or anywhere in the club we haven't seen?" Blade asks.

"I don't think so. Maybe a storage closet or—"

"We need to see everything," I say.

"Theres's a cleaning supplies closet and a booze room in the hallway behind the stage that I don't think you saw. I'll call Gainer then take you to them."

21

———————

While waiting for Ethan and Gainer I continue watching the surveillance footage.

A few guys come by and bring Brook drinks. Some attempt to talk to her, but she doesn't engage. Zoey and Olivia get on the dance floor. Willow continues to wander around. Brook and Harper leave their table again, once again leaving their drinks behind. They go to the restroom. No one approaches the table or appears to place anything in the drinks, but it's a moot point because neither of them return to the table or get their drinks.

The whole club is chaos for the final dance and I lose track of the bridal party, except to see them occasionally popping up in the massive crowd. If it weren't for their TEAM BRIDE sunglasses I probably would't have seen them at all.

I realize that I haven't seen Brook since she went to the restroom, so I go back to that point and concentrate only on the restroom door.

Evidently Brook and Harper weren't the only ones who thought it was a good idea to pee before the final song and closing time because the restrooms are swarmed. I watch closely. There are so many people coming and going I can't be sure, but I don't think Brook comes out of the restroom.

I show Blade.

"So that's where it happened," she says.

"Looks like it."

"Let's take another look at it," she says.

"The restrooms?" Harley says and walks in that direction.

We follow.

As we enter the women's restroom, the lights blink on to reveal the pristine and gleaming surfaces even in the relatively low illumination.

I glance up at the wood plank ceiling and then down and around at the dark stalls and sinks. Then I gaze up at the one foot square window about ten feet up the wall.

"We were so focused on if there was a place to exit the building when we were in here before we didn't look to see if there was a place to hide a body."

Blade turns to Harley. "There any closets or maybe some of those cool secret doors or anything in here?"

She shakes her head. "Nothing."

We look around, feeling along the walls. There are no closets or access panels.

"Did y'all search in here that night?"

Harley shrugs. "Like I said, I think we looked everywhere. We weren't panicking or anything. Nearly every night someone does an Irish Goodbye and their friends don't know where they are, but here's the thing we go through every area to make sure everyone is out as part of our closing and clean up routine."

"Includin' the boss's office and party room?" Blade asks.

"I wish y'all wouldn't call it that," she says. "But *no*, we don't need to because no one goes up there, and he makes sure they're empty before he leaves."

"Is each individual stall searched?" I ask.

"Not only is it checked but it's cleaned, so . . ."

Ethan Cane arrives and we walk back out into the main part of the club to meet him. Matt Gainer walks in just a few minutes later.

"I was brought in on Sunday afternoon," Ethan says, "which was pretty quick considering."

"And don't forget," Harley says. "The bride's best friend was here searching early that morning."

Gainer says, "Yeah, she scared the shit out of me. I squealed like a little girl."

"I guess I was jumpy from—we'd had a few fights the night before and then with a missing girl . . . I was the first one in. Thought I was by myself. Didn't hear her and then suddenly she's right behind me. Wasn't the finest moment for a tough guy, I can tell you that."

Harley says, "We searched that morning too. Wasn't just her. So it's not like Sunday afternoon was the soonest someone searched."

"I had a good scent article," Ethan continues. "If she had been in here we'd've found her, but she wasn't. Two days later we brought in a cadaver dog for the entire building and the surrounding area. I'm tellin' you . . . that young woman is not in this building—and wasn't from the time I did my first search."

"Did the search dog alert on anything?" I ask.

He nods. She definitely was here and we found her scent and followed it around—to her table, the bathroom, the dance floor, then down the escalator, out the front door, and to the Wendy's parking lot."

"You sayin' her ass walked out of here and over to Wendy's and no one saw her and no cameras recorded her?" Blade says.

"Not sayin' that exactly. The dog could've lost the scent. There were a lot of people in here that night. So I'm not sayin' she just strolled out the front door and went and had a hamburger. The only thing I'm sayin' for absolute sure is that she was here that night and she wasn't the next day or two days later—dead or alive."

I turn to Matt Gainer. "How well was the place searched Saturday night?"

"We searched it," he says. "Pretty damn thoroughly. Now, we didn't know we were dealing with a vanishing girl. But we made sure, like we do every night, that no one was left inside the building."

"Could the surveillance footage have been altered?" I ask.

He shakes his large head. "Absolutely not. I'd swear to that under oath in court. I did an offsite backup that night. Downloaded it to an external hard drive and then locked the room. No one knew I did either of those things. If the footage had been doctored it wouldn't match the cloud or the external hard drive copies—and all three are identical."

"That's the thing about this case," Ethan says. "We did all we could and about as early as you could and she's just gone. Here one minute. Gone the next. I don't think she'll ever be found."

22

———

"Why you think the head of security was the first one back in the building the next morning?" Blade asks.

We're on our way back to the office. She's driving and I'm still watching the surveillance footage on my phone.

It appears as if nearly everyone in the club is on the dance floor for the final song of the night. After the song ends, much of the crowd begins to shout for more, but when the DJ gives the final hard no they begin to disperse.

"You'd think a cleaning crew or someone there to receive a delivery, but not the head of security," she adds.

The bridal party drifts toward each other. Most of them have taken off their TEAM BRIDE sunglasses so they're a little more difficult to identify, but Zoey, Harper, and Annabeth still have theirs on and the others are standing with them—everyone but Brook.

The group begins to look around for Brook, searching the club, texting and calling, re-entering the restroom. As far as I can tell no one checks upstairs.

"Since my ass is havin' a conversation with myself," Blade

says, "I'a tell you what I think. I think he went in to erase some of the footage from the night before."

"Sorry," I say. "Trying to finish the surveillance footage. But it is strange that he'd be the first one back in. Probably right about why."

"Need to get a video expert to check the footage," she says. "Or see if the cops or Ben already have."

Eventually, the bridal party, who is being aided in the search by the staff, gives up and leaves. They ride the escalator down and Todd Johns escorts them into the waiting limo.

There's a little footage of the staff cleaning and closing down the place, then Matt Gainer arriving the next morning, unlocking and locking the door, walking up the still escalator.

"It's definitely been edited," I say. "The footage we have is only from certain cameras and only one at a time. And it cuts from the staff closing up to Matt Gainer arriving the next morning. Supposedly this is all the footage that has any relevance to the bridal party—and maybe it is—but it's not even close to all the footage."

"Cops and Ben think they have all the footage," she says. "Question is—*Do they?*"

"If they don't," I say. "If any of the footage has been altered . . . then Chase or his staff are the most likely to have been involved."

"Gotta be Chase," she says. "Head of security not gonna do all this for anybody else."

"'Cept himself," I say.

"True."

"We need to go over every second of all the surveillance footage," I say, "but with all those camera feeds multiplied by all the timeframe we need to examine . . . it'll take weeks—even with some help."

"Maybe we get Ben to hire somebody to do it."

"But will we trust that they did it right?" I ask.

"Probably not," she says. "'Less they find something then we know they did."

I nod. "Probably not a bad place to start."

"What you make of what K-9 dude had to say?" she asks.

"Dog probably got on the wrong scent," I say. "Hard to see her just taking the escalator down and walking out the front door over to Wendy's."

"Maybe she got hungry."

"Why isn't it on the surveillance footage?"

"Gainer wiped it," she says.

"Why? If all she did was walk out of the building, why wipe it?"

"Maybe Chase picked her up over there."

"But we have Wendy's surveillance footage and she's not on it, and neither is Chase. Or any of the other cameras around the area. No way Gainer could wipe all of them."

"So we back to she just up and vanished," she says. "No way we ever find out who took her if we can't figure out *how* it was done or *what actually* happened."

My phone vibrates and I look at the screen.

It's Olivia Lunken, the law student and paralegal, and perhaps the most levelheaded of the bridesmaids.

I answer it.

"I just thought of something," she says. "May not mean anything, but . . . you said tell you anything we think of so . . . You know how everyone says we left Newby's early because the bachelor party was harassing us? Well, that may be true, but . . . they didn't seem to bother Brook nearly as much as this Goth guy who was just hanging out and kind of leering at her. From the moment she saw him she became agitated and ill and . . . I don't know . . . he really bothered her. I think he scared her. Never seen her act like that before. Anyway . . . it's just my opinion but I think that's the real reason she wanted to get out of there. Not the bachelor party. They weren't even in the club or messing with us when she said she wanted to leave."

"They were outside trying to get into your limo."

"They were?"

"Yeah. Driver wouldn't let them."

"Well, then, I'm glad I called. It probably really was the goth guy who made her leave."

"Can you describe him?" I ask.

"Not a chance," she says. "Dark, crowded club. Besides, all that goth shit obscures the person anyway, doesn't it? That's sort of the point, isn't it?"

23

———

Ward Forester is waiting for us at our office.

"How you kids?" he says when we walk in.

He's sitting at our desk, looking at Brook's file.

Ward Forester is an old and old-school PI. He's tough as a galvanized nail and hard as the framing hammer that drives it. He's ruthless and relentless and morally agnostic—equally willing to work for victims and criminals.

Blade says, "Remember that time we told you to always make yourself at home in our office? You don't? That's 'cause we didn't. Put our file down and get out of my chair."

"Oh, it's *your* chair and not *his* chair," he says as he gets up and puts one leg over the front corner of the desk.

Though somewhere between sixty and seventy, Ward looks more like a fit fifty-year-old. Never putting on the excess weight of middle-age, he resembles a retired but still active boxer, his beat-up face and broken nose adding to the illusion.

"What can we do for you, Ward?" I ask.

"Trying to find a couple of missin' girls," he says.

"And you want to hire us to do it for you?" Blade says.

He lets out a bemused laugh lacking warmth and humor.

"Cute. No, not hire you, but I think y'all might be able to help me—at least with one. The first is a young woman from California. Don't expect y'all can help with her, but figured I'd mention her 'cause you never know. She came here on vacation and disappeared. The boyfriend hired me to find her. Name is Hillary York. Know where she is?"

Blade says, "We would if he'd'a hired *us* to find her."

"Well, if you come across the name in your travels . . . I'd appreciate a heads up."

"'Course," Blade says. "Anything we can do to help you would be our pleasure."

"The other is a local girl," he says. "Stepmother hired me to find her. Name's Chrissy Violet. I hear y'all were the last to see her alive and have a good idea where she might be."

"Long as your old ass been doin' this," Blade says, "you'd think you'd be better at it."

"Got a deal for you," he says. "Call it a professional courtesy. I know you kids had a tough time coming up. Feel bad for y'all. Tell me where the body is buried so I can return her to her mom and I'll make sure it does't come back on you. I'll make sure they can never make a case against you."

"That *would* be a sweet deal," Blade says, "*if* we knew where her body was buried and had anything to do with it, but . . . seein' as how we don't and didn't . . . it's a deal we *can* refuse."

"Holla at me you change your mind," he says. "Hate to see either of you do more time. This town's more interesting with you two in it."

24

———————

That night I have Alana.

When I go to search Brook's apartment I take her with me.

Liam, who is still paying for it and says he will until she returns to him, is who gave me both permission and the key.

Now that Blade and I have a better handle on what happened the night of her disappearance, we are broadening our investigation to include, among other things, the victim herself.

Depending upon the person and his or her lifestyle, a victim profile can be extremely helpful in figuring out exactly what happened and who's responsible. Often, the key to unlocking the mystery of someone's disappearance or violent death lies in his or her past. This is far more often the case when the victim's lifestyle is filled with risks and dangerous people—something that is probably not the case for the risk-averse Brook—but we won't know until we look.

For far too long the focus on crime was almost exclusively on the criminal, but more recently forensic experts have come to realize that a greater understanding of victims can help many aspects of society and the criminal justice system, including crime prevention.

We now know that certain risk factors can make a person more likely to become a victim. These factors can be everything from age, sex, race, and income level to living in areas with high levels of transiency and low levels of income and economic opportunity. Two other huge factors are the work one does and the company one keeps. And risk factors change depending on the type of possible crime.

From what I know of Brook she seems to have very few risk factors and yet she became a victim of a crime, so we've got to dig down deeper into her life. It's entirely possible that she was the victim of a random act of violence and that her lifestyle had nothing to do with what happened to her, but we've got to know for sure. We've got to look at every aspect of her life—her past, her family. She seems very risk-averse to me and her choice in boyfriend seems to confirm this assumption but we won't know for sure until we take a closer look at her life. Chances are nothing in Brook's lifestyle, family, past employment, or anything else will have anything to do with what happened to her, but we have to be sure.

Brook has a place in Brookwood Village, a newish, luxurious apartment complex located on Back Beach Road not far from Pier Park.

Though expensive and outwardly ostentatious, her unit is far more stripped down and simple than I expected. The furnishings and decor seem practical, perfunctory, and impersonal, and the only picture in the entire place is a framed 8x10 of her and Liam's engagement photograph, which sits on a mostly empty bookshelf in the living room.

Her furnishings look more like those of a recently divorced dad than a stylish young woman in her early twenties.

Something isn't right here, and I'm immediately suspicious.

Maybe she had already moved most of her things over to

Liam's, but there are no signs of moving at all—no boxes, no packing material or tape.

Though always wanting to play and desiring my constant attention, Alana has recently become far more willing to play alone and entertain herself while I work—as long as it's for short periods of time.

I place the dolls, toys, crayons and coloring books I brought with us on Brook's dining table and place Alana in a chair in front of them.

"You sit here and color and play while I work for a few minutes," I say, "then we'll go get ice cream."

No matter how entertaining she initially finds the items eventually she will wind up watching YouTube videos on my phone.

Without responding to me, she begins to play.

I quickly get to work, knowing I don't have long before she'll require my attention again.

Brook's apartment is immaculate. Neat. Clean. Organized. Nothing is out of place, which is not surprising. But what *is*, is how clean everything is. My guess is either Liam has been periodically coming over to clean or hiring someone to.

The place is so sparse and so tidy I complete my initial cursory search surprisingly quickly.

Her computer is missing. I assume the detectives assigned to her case confiscated it, but I'll need to check. It looks as if they took her bills, banking information, and other paperwork also. I'll check on that also.

"Luc," Alana calls from the living room. "Can I watch your phone?"

"Sure," I say, and as I walk toward her, I unlock my phone, open Youtube, and find a video she likes to watch.

When I hand it to her she starts watching immediately.

"What do you say?" I ask.

"Thank you."

"I'm almost finished," I say. "Just a few more minutes and we'll go grab some ice cream."

"I miss Mommy," she says.

"I know. I'm sorry. She'll be back later tonight."

"Will you tell her to wake me up when she comes in?"

"I'll ask her to," I say.

"Okay. Tell her I said please, please, *please*."

"I will, sweet girl."

While she watches videos on my phone I do a second round of searches, a deeper more invasive search.

This more thorough search produces two suspicious items —suspicious in and of themselves and suspicious because they were hidden.

Inside the secret compartment of a false bottom of a night cream jar in her bathroom I find a stash of foreign, untraceable sim cards, and inside a cookbook safe in the kitchen I find an inordinate amount of pre-paid credit cards.

I hear the front door open and rush into the living room where Alana is.

It's Liam.

He enters slowly, nodding and smiling at me and then Alana.

He's out of uniform, in jeans, flip-flops, and a light-blue Columbian fishing shirt.

"Hope you don't mind," he says. "I couldn't stay away. I miss her so much."

"It's actually good timing," I say. "I have some questions for you."

Alana loses interest and returns to her video.

"Sure," he says. "Anything I can do to help."

He pauses in the middle of the living room and looks around. Shaking his head he says, "Still can't believe she's gone. Probably a fool for keeping up her apartment, but . . . I just . . . can't not. Not until I know for sure she's . . . not coming back."

"I'm surprised by her apartment," I say.

"Oh yeah? How so?"

"How sort of Spartan it is," I say.

He shakes his head slowly. "Sorry, I'm not sure I know what that means."

"She doesn't have a lot of things," I say.

"Oh. She believed in living simply."

"Had she already started moving her things to your place?"

"Not really. She has a few things over there, but . . . just from us being together over the past year, but she hadn't started moving yet."

"The inside of this apartment doesn't go with the outside," I say.

"How do you mean?"

"This is an expensive, luxurious apartment complex," I say. "But the things inside her unit are . . . they're not the kind of things you'd expect at a place like this."

"She wasn't into things," he says. "She really wasn't. She was here at this complex because it's safe and well run."

"What was she into?" I ask.

He seems confused.

"You said she wasn't into things. What was she into?"

"Um, you know . . . just living. She just enjoyed being together. Hanging out. Cooking together. Watching a movie. Going for a walk. Singing. Charades."

"What kind of work did she do?"

"She had a few different online businesses," he says.

"Doing what?"

He shrugs. "Different things. I know she gave lessons."

"What type of lessons?"

"Singing and acting."

Alana lets out a burst of laughter at the video she's watching.

We both turn toward her, but she doesn't even look up.

"What about Brook's family?" I ask when he turns back to face me.

His face clouds over and he frowns and shakes his head. "Her parents were killed in a car crash when she was a junior in high school. She was an only child." His voice wavers a bit and his eyes glisten. "She said she had always felt alone in this world until she met me. Still can't believe she's gone."

"Did she grow up here?" I ask.

He shakes his head. "Missouri. She's been down here for a couple of years."

"What brought her here?"

He smiles and shakes his head. "You know, I'm not sure. She loves the beach so probably that. We didn't get into a lot of stuff from the past. She really practices living in the moment. She used to say the past is a prison."

"I noticed there's no computer here or any personal documents or banking information or bills," I say.

"Investigators took her computer," he says. "She didn't keep that other stuff around. She was a very private person. Shredded her bills after paying them—usually with cash. She had this thing about money and privacy and . . . I don't know . . . It was quirky but I didn't mind. She doesn't have much, lives very modestly, but insisted we have a prenup. I was happy to sign it if it made her feel better, but if for some reason it didn't work between us, and that's something I can't even imagine, I would've taken care of her, given her anything she wanted. She had nothing to fear from me."

25

———

"I'm getting sort of a reputation," Pete is saying. "Everyone's kind of tightlipped around me these days 'cause they know I'm loose-lipped with y'all."

"Not hearin' it from us," Blade says.

It's the next morning and we're having breakfast with Pete at the Waffle House on Thomas Drive.

Pistol Pete Anderson is an investigator with the Bay County Sheriff's Office. He's a clean-cut late-twenties white guy with pale skin and short reddish-blond hair. He was in the system with us when we were kids and is a brother to us. Over the years, he has shared info with us he shouldn't have and it's now coming back to bite him. I just hope not too hard.

"It's not gonna jam you up, is it?" I say.

"I'll be fine."

"Make sure you are," I say. "Don't shoot yourself in the dick for us."

"Sounds like it ain't gonna be an issue if they ain't talkin' to him anymore."

Pete says, "There'll always be people who'll talk. It's just less than it used to be. And it's not our case, so . . . makes it even less. But I still got a little info for you."

As usual, Waffle House is busy and loud—conversations competing with the sounds of cooking and eating, all of which are bouncing around and ricocheting off the hard surfaces of the large, open, tiled-floor room.

Having ordered a la cart, several plates are spread out on the table in front of Pete. Blade's breakfast is confined to a single plate. And I'm just having coffee.

"Your ass gonna get hungry later," Blade says to me. "Wantin' to eat lunch way before I do."

"Probably so."

"If only there was something you could do about that now," she says.

I laugh but say, "Eating when I'm not hungry is not one of them."

Many of us orphans raised by strangers and nursed by the cold, impersonal tit of the state find it difficult to establish and maintain healthy families of our own, and Pete is no exception. A truly decent and kind human being, he seems to be relegated to being a perpetual confirmed bachelor, which makes me sad because I know how much he'd like a family and how much he has to offer one.

"I never miss a chance to eat," he says. "My cupboards stay pretty bare."

"We should go out and grab food more in the evenings," I say.

"Anytime," he says.

I make a mental note to reach out to him more.

"After looking at Brook's apartment," I say. "I get the sense she was hiding—or at least trying to live under the radar or off the grid. Anything in it?"

He nods, finishes chewing, and washes it down with a big

gulp of his Coke. "She was strictly cash and carry. Used pre-paid credit cards, pre-paid phones."

"With foreign, untraceable sim cards," I say.

"She used dummy email accounts and fake business names," he says. "VPN on all her internet activity. Mail drop service. Didn't help them find her, but they also found out she changed her identity a few years back. And she must've used a very elite service to do it because it's good. After all the searching and investigating . . . best they could come up with is that she has a new identity, but they couldn't tell who she was before."

Blade looks at me with raised eyebrows. "If she had just changed her name . . . it'd be public record and we'd know who she was before."

"She went to some extreme trouble and expense to truly get a new life," I say.

"Witness protection?" Blade says.

I shrug. "Possibly. Or domestic abuse."

"More likely," she says with a frown.

I look back at Pete, who is continuing to shovel food into his mouth, but before I can say anything our waitress, a large black woman who looks like she could be Lizzo's mom, walks up and says, "Get y'all anything else?"

Pete looks at us. As usual, when we pump him for info we're paying.

We both nod.

"Another order of crispy bacon and a pecan waffle please," he says.

"Sure thing, sweetie. Comin' up."

"How thoroughly was her fiancé and bridesmaids looked into?" I ask.

"Thoroughly," he says. "They're all clean. Not a record among them. And their statements check out. Fiancé only has a friend for an alibi, but both are in law enforcement and have the respect of their colleagues and commanders."

"Do you know how closely the surveillance footage was examined?" I ask.

"Very," he says. "She did not come out of that bar. Everyone was accounted for. They tracked everyone who went in and logged when they came out. She's the only one who went in and didn't come out."

"How about the footage itself?" I ask.

"It's legit," he says. "Not altered. Not edited. The forensic lab FDLE sent it to says so."

"And that's the fuckin' kicker," Blade says. "She didn't come out of the building. She ain't still in the building. She ain't in the walls or at Wendy's. Doesn't matter what her real identity is if we can't figure out what the hell happened to her and where the hell she is."

26

"Your client's fiancé ain't who she appeared to be," Blade says.

"Who is?" Ben says.

"Don't just mean they's a difference in her public and private persona," she says. "She ain't who she claimed to be."

"That's good," he says. "More reasonable doubt if he gets indicted. Did her identity have anything to do with her disappearance?"

"Not sure yet," I say. "Hard to imagine it didn't in someway. She went to extreme effort and expense to become someone else."

"We can track her other identity by her name change petition or her social security number."

"Wasn't a public records name change," I say. "It's not public at all. And she changed everything—name, social, birth certificate, all her documents."

"No way," he says.

"*Way*," Blade says.

"That's . . . nearly impossible."

"Nearly," I say.

"And extremely expensive. She'd have to have a lot of hidden liquidity."

"No wonder she wanted a prenup," I say.

"And not something you can do legally," he says.

"True," I say.

For someone to legally change their identity, they usually start by changing their name, which is a matter of public record and can be traced. They often then move to a different location, use cash, which they would need a lot of, abandon all social media and their old phones, computers, and other devices, drop all friends, family, and other contacts, and use a mail drop service. If they have tremendous willpower and are fully committed they usually change their appearance by gaining or losing weight, dying their hair, and completely changing their style of clothing.

None of this is easy—especially to sustain—and it's almost all trackable. We've found many people over the years who attempted to disappear employing some or even all of these tactics.

"Unless . . . Think she's part of some kind of federal witness protection program?"

"Maybe," I say, "but it's hard to see. She's so young and . . . just doesn't seem like the kind of person who would be in organized crime or anything else needing witness protection."

"But that could just be a new persona."

"She is an actress," I say. "But still hard to see. We've got to assume that everything she told Liam and everyone else isn't true—parents dead, from Missouri, all that kind of stuff."

"Wonder if she told anyone who she really is?" Ben says.

"Be hard not to," Blade says.

"I've been looking into the companies that offer this service," I say. "It's amazing what a big industry it is. Especially in Japan. It's so popular over there they have a name for it. They call people who purposefully vanish from their lives *jouhatsu*.

It's a Japanese word that means evaporation. Most do it for the reasons you'd expect—legal issues, huge debt, wanting to end a relationship. They call the operation night moving."

"Night moving," Blade says, shaking her head. "We did a shit ton of that as kids, didn't we?"

"Yes, we did," Ben says.

"This catches on . . . it's the end to skip tracing," Blade says. "We can kiss that part of our business goodbye."

Ben, who is looking at his phone, says, "I just pulled up one of these companies in North America. It's called Vanesco International and is a consulting firm and information provider on nationality and residency placements. Says they provide services and advice for various issues related to new identities, second passports/citizenships, and anonymous travel. Looks like 'vanesco' is Latin for vanish, disappear, pass away. They work with the governments of certain countries where American and Canadian citizens can relocate as part of their vanishing act. But that's not the same as creating a completely new identity for someone staying in their own country, is it? Their website says they've been in business for over sixty years, acting as a referral agent using an association of international lawyers and specialists in order to provide the most private and up-to-date services, all protected by the attorney client privilege."

"If this company sends our vanishing citizens to other countries," I say, "is it possible that companies in other countries send their vanishing citizens here?"

Ben says, "I'd say it's highly likely."

"But," Blade says, "this bitch don't seem foreign. Nobody said anything about her accent or mannerisms or—"

"That's true," I say, "but we didn't ask them."

"Well, I think we should," she says.

27

That evening we have an impromptu gathering of the bridesmaids. Everyone but Harper is able to attend.

We're at a table on the upper deck of Uncle Ernie's, the setting sun sinking into St. Andrews Bay and reflecting a shimmering path of light on the gently rocking surface of the water.

The sunset is breathtaking and provides a stunningly brilliant and beautiful backdrop to the dark undulating waters of the bay.

"We're trying to get a better understanding of Brook," I say.

"Why?" Olivia Lunken asks. "This better not be about blaming the victim."

The smooth caramel skin of her face is tight, her body rigid, her harsh tone prosecutorial.

"Not at all," I say. "We'd never do that. She's blameless. All victims are. No, all we want to do is understand her better. Too much focus is placed on criminals and cases and law enforcement instead of victims."

Olivia relaxes a little but still appears unconvinced.

The day is done but the night has yet to come. We're in the

magic part of evening that has that calm, airy quality, which is only enhanced by being near the bay at sunset.

"What can y'all tell us about her?"

"She was an angel," Zoey Wanamaker says. "A real sweetheart. At least most of the time."

I can hear in her use of the words *angel* and *sweetheart* the echoes of her using them with her students in her classroom. Perhaps even when she doesn't mean them.

"She always reminded me of a movie star," Poppy Paterson says. "She had that thing, that star quality."

She says this as if she knows all about it because she has it too.

"She did," Zoey says, "but she never . . . she was never arrogant or stuck up. She was still so sweet. At least most of the time."

"But it could've been that special charisma, that glow she had that made her . . . that caused a psychopath to notice her," Willow adds.

Tonight Willow's pale, reddish-tinted skin looks even lighter, but the freckles that fleck it look darker somehow.

Across the way, on the opposite side of the deck, a friend of mine, Josh Tucker, is playing a solo acoustic set, and his soft, soothing song selection is the perfect accompaniment for the mellow moment we're all experiencing.

"Where'd she grow up?" I ask.

"Missouri, wasn't it?" Poppy says.

Zoey nods. "It was."

"How long had she been in Panama City?" I ask. "What brought her here?"

"Past few years," Zoey says. "No idea what bought her here though."

"What can you tell us about her family?"

"Not much," Olivia says. "She was an only child and her parents were killed in a car accident years ago."

"Any of you ever notice her having a hint of a foreign accent?"

"*What?*" Zoey asks. "No. What in the world?"

"What is this?" Olivia says, and I can hear in her words the authority and indignation she's going to have in the courtroom one day.

"Just questions," I say. "What can you tell me about the work she did?"

Poppy says, "She gave online lessons for singers and actors. She was not just extremely talented but a very good teacher too."

"What about other friends besides y'all?"

They don't know of any.

"How about any ex-boyfriends?" I say. "Anyone she was seeing before Liam?"

None of them know of any.

"Are you trying to say we didn't know Brook as well as we think we did?" Olivia asks.

"Objection," I say. "Calls for speculation."

She smiles.

"We ain't *tryin'* to say anything," Blade says. "We're tryin' to gather information. That's what we do, how we find missin' people."

I add, "We never know what's important or if anything is. We just have to keep asking questions, knocking on doors, turning over stones. It's the only way we know how to do what we do."

Zoey says, "Harper might know. She was closer to Brook than anybody."

28

"Now's not a good time," Harper says.

She has just unlocked the door of her closed downtown art gallery where she's working alone.

"This won't take long," I say.

We push past her into the little boutique gallery of bland beach scene watercolors.

After leaving the other bridesmaids, we decided to pay her a surprise visit and go at her hard.

Finding her alone in her gallery is perfect.

"Why weren't you there tonight?" I ask.

"Had to work late," she says. "Sorry."

"*Had* to?" Blade asks, looking around at the small gallery that looks exactly the same as the last time we were here.

"I don't think you ever *have* to do anything," she says.

"We thought you were serious about wanting to find your friend," I say.

"I am."

"Just not enough to actually show up and help us," Blade says.

"I wanted to, I just—" She's growing nervous and agitated. "I'll help you now. What do you want to know?"

"What you're hiding," I say.

"*Hiding*?"

"Yeah," I say. "You're supposed to be Brook's best friend, but you're not helping us much or giving us the information we need to find her."

Her smooth, round, photogenic face clouds over. I think she's about to cry, but her bright blue eyes don't glisten.

"I am," she says. "I thought I was."

"I think you didn't come tonight 'cause you didn't want the other bridesmaids to see you were lying."

"What? No. About what?"

"About who Brook really was," I say.

The quick widening of her eyes and the recognition in her pale face reveals we're right about her knowing.

"What do you mean?" she asks. "I've told you who she was."

Her words are shaking and unconvincing.

"Can we continue this tomorrow?" she says. "I'm not feeling well and need to go home."

Her breathing is erratic and she seems on the verge of panic.

"We gonna finish it right now," Blade says.

"I need to sit down," she says.

Her knees buckle and she starts to collapse.

I grab her and Blade grabs a chair and we lower her into it.

"We know you know," I say.

"Know what? Can I have some water?"

"Sure," Blade says. "Soon as you tell us the truth. Water is for truth tellers."

"Are you the only one who knows?" I ask. "Does Liam?"

"Knows what?" she says.

"That Brook—or whoever she is—changed her entire identity."

She sinks back into the chair and looks a little relieved. "How did you—"

"It's our job," I say. "Who else knows?"

"No one," she says. "I'm the only one. No one else has a clue."

"Including Liam?"

She nods. "No one else knows. How much do you know?"

Blade says, "Act like we don't know shit and tell us everything."

"Why'd she do it?" I ask.

"To escape the vilest, sickest, most evil man on the planet," she says. "And I'm afraid he found her anyway."

"Who is the vilest, sickest, most evil man on the planet?" Blade asks. "I feel like that's something I need to know."

"Raven," she says.

"*Raven*?" Blade says. "Raven have a last name?"

"The shock rocker?" I ask.

She nods.

And all the pieces fall into place.

"Is she Hillary York?" I ask.

She nods.

"Who?" Blade asks. "Isn't that who Ward is looking for?"

"The child actress," I say, nodding. "Got her break in that Disney show, then starred in Family Fortune."

"Must be some white people shit," Blade says.

"It is," I say.

"She was nominated for an Oscar in her one and only film role as an abused thirteen year-old who becomes a sex worker and drug addict. Shortly thereafter she started seeing Raven. They became a couple and were together for a few years before they had a highly publicized horrible break up. It came out that he had been extremely abusive and violent. He did some very sick shit to her for a very long time. Shortly after the break up and all this becoming public she disappeared. It was suspected that he or one of his many demented fans killed her, but no evidence was ever found."

29

———

Hillary Brooks York is an American actress, activist, model, and singer. She has been nominated for an Oscar, two Critic's Choice Awards, three Emmys, and two People's Choice Awards. Best known for her role in the television series *Family Fortune*, she was nominated for an Oscar for her work on *Subway* in which she played a troubled teen sex worker. She dated shock rocker Raven for most of her adolescence. Following their breakup, she alleged that he was abusive and disappeared shortly thereafter. Where is Hillary York and did Raven, aka Shawn Johnson, or his fans have anything to do with her disappearance?

Blade and I are back in our office reading about and watching clips related to Hillary York and Raven LuRue.

"He started grooming me when I was fourteen and he was thirty-four," Hillary is saying. "I was a child. He was a grown man approaching middle age. He brainwashed me. He coerced me. He gaslit me. At the time I thought it was . . . this . . . I don't know . . . once-in-a-lifetime love affair. I thought he was so cool. I thought most of his horrible behavior was an act, a persona. I was wrong. He systematically and horrifically abused me for years. He had me tattoo his name on me, but then that wasn't enough so then he had me carve his name into my flesh and made me drink his blood. I was a teenager searching for an identity. I had recently lost my mom, and my dad wasn't around much. My career was taking off and no one was looking out for me. I was doing these sexual scenes with co-stars twice my age. I was working all the time. I had been taken out of school. I no longer had time to hang out with my friends. I was isolated and . . . vulnerable. He became my everything. He separated me from everyone. He insisted on complete control and domination. He convinced me we weren't like everyone else. They were blind and boring and sleeping through life, but we were awake, alive, tuned into the true power of alternative living, of true love. He drugged me. He raped me. He tortured me. He controlled me. He belittled me. He has threatened me. His fans are sending me death threats. And I have little doubt he or they will do it given the chance, but I can't be silent anymore. I have to speak my truth and live my freedom even if it gets me killed."

"No wonder she wanted a prenup," I say. "She was rich. And had the resources to run."

Blade says, "No wonder she freaked out when she saw the goth guy at the club."

I nod.

"His freaky little followers are like an army," she adds. "I've been lookin' at their little fanboy sites. It feels like a cult. They'll do anything for him. It's like the little bitches who stormed the Capitol or flew the planes into the towers or walked into a mall with an AK. It's so sick and sad and pathetic. He is their . . . everything and many of them say they'd happily kill her for him."

"Sheeple needing a cause," I say. "Something to give them purpose and meaning. They become soldiers in the cult of celebrity. Like religion or politics. Same sick shit at work."

"I continue to suffer from severe PTSD," York is saying. I

struggle with OCD, depression, addiction. I am traumatized beyond what I can begin to describe, but I'm a survivor. I am surviving. It's important to understand that he started off slowly. For those of you who ask why did you put up with this, why didn't you just leave, it was like boiling a frog. If you throw a frog in a pot of boiling water, it will hop right back out, but if you put a frog in a pot of room temperature water and slowly warm it up over time until it's boiling the frog will stay in and boil to death. Predators know how to do what they do, and the more they do it the better they get at it. Again, I was a child. He was twenty years older than me. I was not his first victim. I wasn't his last, but whoever is at this moment my sincere hope is she will be his last. His toxic emotional, psychological, mental, physical, and sexual abuse didn't start at the boiling point. It started barely above room temperature then escalated over time as he was more and more in control of my entire life and had isolated me from all my family and friends. Nothing was off limits. Nothing was out of bounds. We had no boundaries. We had no limits. And everything was a test of my limits, everything was to push my tolerance. He totally dominated me. I was his property, his child, his slave, his fuck doll, and I can't tell you how many times I woke up to the man who claimed to be the only one who understood or cared for or loved me raping what he thought was my unconscious body."

"You ever listen to any of his music?" Blade asks.

"Not on purpose," I say. "But I've encountered it over the years—especially clips of his videos."

Raven LuRue, who now just goes by Raven, is one of the most controversial figures in heavy metal music and shock rock. His lyrics and the images in his videos and shows depict violence, degradation of women, racism, fascism, Nazism, homophobia, animal sacrifice, and the like. Several murderers and rampage shooters, especially those of the teenage school shooting variety have cited Raven as an inspiration.

"The louder the screaming and the more extreme the antics the less the talent," I say. "Plus it's not my kind of music."

"You'd think with all the rage inside your white ass you'd love that shit."

"You would."

"But you listen to all that deep, angsty singer-songwriter shit to try and quiet the beast within."

"He released a statement through his management following York going public and his record company dropping him," I say. "'I'll never apologize for what I do. I'm an artist and artists are always attacked by inferior minds who don't understand. My misunderstood art and even my very existence have always been controversial to the simpleminded. But know this. Ms. York's claims about me are completely false and truly terrible exaggerations and distortions of what actually happened. Everything I have ever done, and I mean *ever*, have always been completely consensual. I wrongly thought Ms. York was a kindred spirit partner. I was wrong. Now she is trying to revive her dead career by using my celebrity, and I hope you can all see through it.'"

Blade says, "I's more interested in the *Rolling Stone* interview he gave about it where he said 'Every single day I fantasize about crushing her skull in by stomping on her head with my boots.'"

"What a sweetheart."

"Not long after that his publicist released a statement saying the comment was 'clearly a nonliteral, hyperbolic, theatrical, and playful statement by a rock god promoting a new project.'"

I shake my head.

"Man," she says, shaking her head too. "White people. Am I right?"

I nod my agreement. "You are right."

"So," she says, "she finally breaks up with him. Takes some

time to heal or whatever but what she's really doing is using her child star TV money to buy a new identity. She comes out and tells everybody what a—surprise, surprise—monster he is and then disappears."

"Something like that, yeah," I say, "and he's investigated in connection with her disappearance."

"Sweet."

"That *is* a nice touch," I say. "And he's been telling anybody who'll listen that he's not only innocent of the abuse allegations but of her disappearance. And if he's a proactive guy he's probably been searching for her."

"Hiring private dicks like Ward," she says. "But wonder how he traced her to Panama City?"

"Wonder what brought her here in the first place," I say. "She may have had a connection he knew about. Probably did. Think about how similar her new name is to her old one. Her subconscious probably guided her to the familiar and comfortable even as she thought she was doing new and random things. If not, then he probably heard the story of the disappearing bride and saw a picture of her. She's older now and she changed her appearance, but maybe he recognized her."

"Say he or his little fanboys had something to do with her disappearance," she says. "Still doesn't tell us how."

"No, it doesn't," I say. "But . . . what if the goth guy at Newby's, who was obvious with his presence and leering, was there to try to get her to leave early. Plan could've been to get her back to Jungle Jim's all along."

"Like maybe he got a fanboy who works there or some connection to Chase," she says.

"Could—"

Lexi appears at our door and I stop.

"Sorry to just drop by," she says.

"This professional or personal?" Blade asks. "Professional and you don't have to apologize."

She smiles. "Personal."

Though I'm nearly almost happy to see her, it bothers me that Lexi has just dropped by, and I feel her presence as an intrusion. And I wonder why.

Is it because I'm so focused on the case? Because we've just found out who Brook really is and who might be behind her disappearance and it's our best lead so far or is it something else?

I realize that I want Lexi around when it's convenient for me and I really want to see her but am bothered by her just showing up and not asking ahead of time.

I also realize it has something to do with Heather Harrison and what might be developing between us.

"Come on in," I say. "We should probably wrap up for the night anyway. Have you eaten?"

Before she can respond Cindi Rush runs in.

"Well, hell now," Blade says, "we got enough for a double date."

"I'm so sorry," Rush says. "I . . . I'm weak and . . ."

Blade nods her head like she has been expecting this.

"They broke me," she says.

"It's . . . what I expected," Blade says.

"There wasn't much I could tell them," she says. "Don't know anything about what happened after you dropped me off, but . . . I did tell them you took her to kill her. I'm so sorry. I love you. I really do. I'm just weak and . . . I—"

Bob Kirkland walks in with two uniforms who tower over his short, middle-aged frame.

"I see she's already told you," he says.

Blade says, "Told me she didn't have much to tell you."

"We're hoping you'll fill in the gaps for us," he says.

He yawns and rubs his head, mussing the halo of closely cropped gray hair there. He's gloating and seems to take no pleasure in what he's doing.

Rush says, "I'm so sorry, baby. I—"

Blade looks at her. "Part of me thought you might be the one, but part of me knew you'd do this. And I had to know. They've got nothin' on me. I'll be out soon. Have all your shit out of my place before I get back."

Kirkland says, "Will you come have a conversation with me or do I have to arrest you?"

"Sure, I'll talk to you, Bob."

"I'll call Ben," I say.

"No need," Blade says. "I got this. I'll be in touch with you. And Burke, thank you, brother. For everything. You the only one in this whole damn world I can count on."

30

———

"How worried are you?" Lexi asks.

"Scale from one to ten, 'bout a thirty," I say.

Ignoring what Blade had said, I had called Ben and knowing he's at the police station with her makes me feel better, but I'm still worried.

The two of us are alone in our office. I'm pacing around the room trying to walk out some of my nervous energy.

"What can I do? Make some dinner? Take you to dinner? Take you out drinking? Want to talk? What?"

She's trying to be helpful and though I appreciate the effort it's not helping.

I shake my head. "I don't think there's anything you can do."

"Some really good sex would take your mind off it," she says.

"You're probably right but I can't—not with her in custody and . . ."

I realize that what I want to be doing is talking to Heather, having her calm, melancholic presence comfort me.

"I think I need to be alone," I say. "Need to sort some things out and figure my next move."

"You sure?" she asks.

I nod.

"Okay," she says, her voice full of disappointment. "Call me if you change your mind. I know I can help you if you let me."

"Thank you," I say. "If I can think of anything at all I'll call you."

"You better," she says.

When she is gone, I call Ben again, but he doesn't answer.

A few moments later he texts me back.

Relax. I'm on this. I'll call when I know something.

I try to read more about Hillary York and Raven LuRue but I'm too worked up, too anxious about Blade. I find myself reading the same paragraph over and over several times and still not knowing what it says.

After giving up on the reading, I attempt to occupy my mind by figuring out how Raven or his minions might have taken Brook. It always comes back to that—how could it have been done? Eyewitnesses and surveillance footage says she walked into Jungle Jim's and never walked out again. And that's true and has to be answered even if Raven and a small army of his followers were involved.

Eventually, I give up and call Heather.

"Made me so happy to see your name pop up on my phone," she says.

"What're you doing?"

"Having a quiet drink alone at Dave's."

"Up for some bad company?" I ask.

"Absolutely," she says. "It's my favorite kind."

31

D ave's Corner Pub is a nice quiet place to have a drink. There's no band, no jukebox, no pool tables or dart machines. The only sounds are those of quiet conversations to the soft soundtrack of the barely audible Postmodern Jukebox station on the house speakers.

It's dim but not dark. It's small but not overly crowded. Its clientele skews older and mellower than any other watering hole in town.

I find her alone at the end of the bar sipping on a tall glass of Chardonnay.

When I walk up to her she stands and gives me an enthusiastic hug, holding it for a long moment.

"What can I get you?" the bartender asks.

He's a large middle-aged man with thick, straight hair, a big bushy beard, and a white bar towel slung over his left shoulder.

"Something with vodka and some kind of juice."

He nods and begins working on it.

"Let's go in the backroom," she says.

There are only a handful of customers in the establishment and none of them are in the small backroom.

"Sounds good," I say.

We take our drinks and walk into the little semi-secluded area in the back. It's an odd, open room with booths around the edges—probably a pool room in an earlier life.

We sit in the very back booth, which is the most private place in the entire bar.

She doesn't ask how I'm doing or what's wrong, just waits for me to talk in my own time, but the full weight of her attention is on me.

"Blade was arrested tonight," I say.

She shakes her head and frowns and says, "I'm so sorry."

Reaching across the table, she puts her hand on mine.

We sip our drinks slowly, and I can feel myself beginning to calm down some. Her hand on mine helps.

Taking my time, I tell her about Chrissy Violet's disappearance, our involvement, and Kirkland's investigation.

"So . . . that happened while you were searching for Leah," she says.

I nod.

"Can't believe you were having to deal with that while doing all you were doing for us," she says. "The work you do . . . it's . . . so difficult and dangerous. You help so many people—like me —but the . . . cost involved is . . . so high."

Rush asked for our help with her ex who was stalking and harassing her, but the reason we took the case was Blade's interest in her, which soon resulted in a relationship, so it's complicated and cloudy as to how much of it was work and how much personal. And either way Blade's extreme response to Violet's kidnapping, imprisonment, and assault of her and Rush had nothing to do with the work we do.

"Most of it is the work," I say, "but some of it's lifestyle."

"I'd think it'd take a certain type of person with a certain lifestyle to be able to do the work."

I nod. "Probably. But . . . we could do without my issues with rage and Blade's obstinate pride."

"You're so . . . gentle," she says. "It's hard to imagine you bein' violent."

"I work hard to keep the beast in the cage."

We finish our drinks.

"Would you like another?" she asks. "Here or . . . somewhere else? I have vodka and juice at my place."

"Yeah, let's get out of here."

We take our empty glasses back to the bar, settle our tab, and head for the door.

Just as we reach the door, a gaunt, drunk, unkempt old man stumbles in and bumps into Heather.

I reach out attempting to block him with one arm and pull her back with the other, but I'm a moment too late.

"Watch where you're goin' bitch," he yells.

With my arm that's already extended, I backhand him away from us.

I turn toward her. "You okay—"

He careens into a large wooden coat rack and either inadvertently knocks it or purposefully shoves it toward me. The solid, heavy, hard top of the rack strikes me in the back of the head and all my frustration and anger and rage erupts.

The old familiar shift happens inside me and I'm powerless to do anything about it.

Kicking the old man through the door, I grab the coat rack. Lifting it up and using it like a battering ram I swing it around in an attempt to break things.

Unleashing my fury I knock framed photos and posters down, glass shattering on the scarred wooden floor. After stabbing several holes in the sheet rock wall, I begin to bang the coat rack on the floor, damaging the floor and busting apart the coat rack.

It's several moments before I become aware of what I've

done and begin to hear both the bartender and Heather's voices.

"Luc," Heather is saying, her voice calm but persistent. "Luc. Luc, stop."

The bartender has stopped yelling and I see that he is on the phone.

"No," I say, turning toward him. "Don't call the cops. I'll pay for everything. I'll—"

"They're already on their way," he says. "And you better not try to run. I've got your credit card info."

"I'm so sorry," I say. "I just . . ."

I step through the door to check on the old man as the bartender yells, "Get the fuck back in here."

The old man isn't hurt too badly. He has some abrasions on his hands and face and will be sore tomorrow, but he's okay.

I reach down and offer him a hand up.

"Stay the fuck away from me," he says.

Then Heather is there helping him up and back into the bar.

Inside, I walk over to the bartender. "I'm so sorry about that. Would you please just let me pay for it and not involve cops. I'm on probation and if I get—"

"Should'a thought about that before you decided to go crazy and break shit."

"He's going through a lot right now," Heather says. "Please just let us pay for the damages. We'll pay you double what it'll cost you to fix it. Please."

"It's out of my hands. Cops are on the way. Now have a seat over there in the corner and leave everyone alone."

As we move over to take a seat he makes his way down to where the old man is sitting at the bar. "You're okay, Charles. Nothing that a few drinks on the house can't fix."

"Free drinks," Charles says. "Hit me some more."

"I'm goin' back to prison," I say to Heather.

"Isn't there anything we can do?"

"You can go," I say. "You don't have to stick around for this. You didn't do anything wrong."

"I'm not going anywhere. But I want to help you. I just don't know how."

I realize I have one chance of getting out of this and though I don't want to do it I have no choice but to call Lexi.

32

———

"What the fuck, Luc?" Lexi is saying.

"I just lost it."

We are standing out in front of Dave's, the flashing lights of the cop car bathing everything in blue. Everyone else is inside the bar.

"I'm not even talkin' about that," she says. "We'll get to that. I mean . . . you send me away and less than an hour later I find you out with another woman at a bar."

"It's Leah's mom—"

"I know who it is."

"I was just waiting for word from Ben," I say. "Wanted a quiet place to have a drink."

I'm trying to imply I just happen to run into Heather without out and out lying, hoping she won't ask me directly.

"Place was quiet," she says. "'Til you went all rock star hotel room on it."

"I got hit in the back of the head and everything just . . . the beast was unleashed. Didn't realize what I was doing until it was mostly over."

"The fuck you got against coat racks?"

She is taking all this far better than I expected, and I'm grateful she's not causing a scene or making things worse.

"I'm sorry," I say. "I really am."

"What would've happened if the old man hadn't been outside when you went berserk but right in front of you? Would you have bashed his head in?"

"I certainly hope not. Maybe some part of me knew to kick him out front so he'd be safe."

"A little Jekyll left beneath all that Hyde?"

"Maybe. Hopefully."

"Are you two seeing each other?" she asks. "Sleeping together?"

I shake my head.

"You know she's nearly old enough to be your mother," she says, then her eyes widen and her mouth drops open a little. "She . . . You . . . You're an orphan and she lost a child."

"Please don't," I say. "Not now."

"It helps me understand it better. It really does."

"We were just talking," I say.

"From what I gather you were leaving together," she says. "I mean, what the fuck? I was just with you. You said you'd tell me if you started seeing anyone."

"I'm not seeing her," I say.

"We need to talk about us and what this means, but for now . . . you're not going back to prison."

"Thank you so much," I say.

"I talked to the cops and the bartender and worked everything out. Bartender has a nephew on probation, and I told him I'd help him out some if I could. Cops are happy about not having to arrest you and the paperwork that would involve. And you have to pay for all the damages."

I nod. "Absolutely. Anything. Thank you. I really, really appreciate you doing all this for me."

"You're lucky I'm not a vindictive bitch," she says. "Finding you here with another woman after you sent me home less than an hour ago. I could've made this a lot worse on you. But I care about you, Luc. I hate to see the way you sabotage yourself. I know you're worried about Blade. I know you've got Logan and Dimitri comin' at you. I know you're frustrated about not finding that bride, but . . . those aren't and can't be excuses. And you are your own worst enemy. You're doin' far more to hurt yourself than Logan or Dimitri are."

"I know."

"You gotta get your shit together," she says. "Your nine lives are running out."

"I will. I'm trying. Thank you for all your help. I really appreciate it."

"Just do better and pay for the damages. Oh, and don't come back here. You're banned for life."

We walk back inside.

The cops are wrapping up and leaving.

"See you 'round, Lexi," one of them says, and I can tell by the way he looks at her he's interested.

"Thanks again, fellas," she says. "I owe you."

"We're gonna collect," he says. Turning to me he says, "Thanks to the best probation officer in the state you got a second chance. Don't blow it."

"I won't," I say. "And thank y'all very much."

"Didn't do it for you, loser," he says, and they walk out.

The bartender says, "I'll get with Dave and we'll get an estimate for the repairs in a day or two."

"As soon as you have it I'll be up here with the money."

"You better be or the deal is off."

"He will be," Lexi says. "You have my word."

"What about me?" the old man asks. "What do I get?"

"Free drinks, Charles," the bartender says. "Your favorite thing."

When everything has been concluded, Lexi, Heather, and I walk out front.

Once outside we pause and I can tell both of them are waiting to see what I'm going to do, each with the expectation it will be with them. It's an awkward moment, one I can't figure a way out of—until I decide to fake a phone call.

I pull my phone out of my pocket and take a few steps away while I pretend to take a call.

"That was Ben," I lie when I step back over to them. "I've got to go meet with him. I want to apologize again to both of you and thank you for your understanding and kindness. I'm very ashamed and very sorry."

I rush toward my car, thankful I met Heather here instead of us coming together.

As I flee like a coward into the night, I see that they stand there a little longer and engage in conversation, and I wonder what they must be saying.

I quickly conclude I'm probably better off not knowing.

33

———————

Later that night, I got a call from Ben then Blade.

Ben says, "They arrested her. I tried to get them not to, but . . . they're just frustrated and wanting to do something. I'm sure they're hoping it will rattle her, but she's not rattled."

"She doesn't," I say.

"They have no case," he says. "They're overreaching beyond what I've ever seen before. No body. No murder weapon. No evidence. No eyewitness to the crime."

"Can you get the judge to dismiss it?" I ask.

"I'll certainly bring a motion to, but she hasn't even had first appearance yet. So . . . it won't be quick. Anyway, we can discuss everything tomorrow. I'll know more then. I just wanted to let you know what's going on and tell you that she'll be calling you in a few. She gets one phone call and it's got to be brief. I wanted you to be expecting it. Be sure to answer."

"Will do," I say. "I'll see you in the morning. And thanks for everything."

"Don't thank me yet," he says. "I should've been able to keep her from getting arrested, but . . . I'll see if I can't fix this sooner rather than later."

A call from the jail comes in, and I end the call with him to take it.

"Don't have long," she says. "I'll make this fast. I need a favor."

"Name it."

"I was hopin' it wouldn't come to this. Never should have. But these bitches be jumpin' the gun like mofos, man. Just didn't expect everything to go down this fast. I didn't mean for it to come to this. Didn't think it would. And I bet it wouldn't have if I less pigmentation and a penis."

"Wait. You don't have a *penis*?"

"Remember that crazy chick we found back before you got popped?"

"Yeah."

"Remember where we took her?"

"Yeah?"

"Need you to go there tomorrow."

"Okay."

"They tellin' me I got to get off," she says.

"What do you want me to do when I get there?"

"You'll know what to do," she says.

"Okay. I'll leave first thing in the morning."

"See you when you get back. And, Burke."

"Yeah?"

"Thanks, man. Thanks for always havin' my back. Thanks for always bein' on my side—even when it's the wrong side."

Early the next morning, Lexi and I strike out for Apalachicola.

I had intended to take the hour drive alone, but she asked if she could go and if we could talk on the way and I couldn't think of a good reason to say *no*.

We take Highway 98 along the coast through Mexico Beach and Port St. Joe, the scenic landscape alternating between pinewood flatland forests and the sparkling sun-kissed emerald-green waters of the Gulf of Mexico.

"Will you tell me where you're at?" she says. "I mean with us."

I nod. "But before I do let me say again how much I appreciate not only what you did last night but the way you handled everything. It was very . . . It showed a lot about your character and it meant more to me than I can tell you."

She smiles. "It's the reason I'm in this car with you this morning, isn't it?"

I smile back at her. "Didn't hurt. That's for sure. That's the thing about a relatively new relationship—and even those that aren't so new. Everything that happens, every reaction to every-thing that happens—especially the difficult and challenging things—is an opportunity. Character is revealed. Trust either built or destroyed."

She nods. "So I built back some trust last night after destroying it by the way I responded to the photos Logan sent me."

"Blade keeps talkin' about people passin' or failing tests," I say. "I understand what she's sayin', but I don't see this that way. I'm not doing anything to test you and I don't feel like you are with me, but life and circumstances test us all the time. If last night was a test that life administered to us, I failed and you passed."

"Because I helped you out of a jam instead of being petu-lant and punishing you for being there with another woman."

I smile again. "Because you were . . . Yeah, something like that."

"Can we talk about that other woman?"

"Let's talk about us," I say.

She nods. "Fair enough."

"I believe we have some real chemistry and a genuine connection," I say. "I'm very attracted to you and I care for you deeply."

"But?" she says.

"But I'm your probationer. You're my probation officer. That's always hanging over us. We can't ever be truly free to . . . We can't fully and freely explore what a real relationship between us would be like because we're not fully free to do so. It handicaps us—and has from the very beginning."

She nods and lets out a big sigh. "You're . . . It's true."

"The thing is . . . I really like what we have. Hanging out together and with Alana. And our sex is . . . fantastic. But part of our hanging out is hiding out. So . . . and I don't think I've ever thought about it this way exactly, but . . . I . . . because of all the limitations on us, the . . . parameters we have to exist in . . . I haven't let myself go all in and I don't think you have either."

She seems to think about it, twisting her lips and then very slowly nodding her agreement. "I think that's true. But I think I may be . . . I may have let myself go farther in than you have."

I shrug. "Not sure about that, but . . . this is . . . You asked where I'm at . . . I think this is where we are."

"I think you're right."

"And here's the . . . Is what we have enough? Can it be for two more years?"

She doesn't respond, and the existential questions of our very relationship linger, hovering in the space between us for the rest of the trip.

Apalachicola is a fishing village turned touristy town where the Apalachicola River empties into the Apalachicola Bay. It's a small town with some old buildings and interesting architecture where shrimp boats return at sunset. Before collapsing because of the lack of flow of the river and overpopulation and overfishing, the bay once produced nearly ninety percent of Florida oysters.

As we pull into town, Lexi says, "Where are we going again?"

"Maddie Marie's," I say. "It's a sort of secretive treatment facility and halfway house. Not many people know about it. It's controversial but effective at helping addicts and others with mental healing and health. We only know about it because we did some work for Maddie a few years ago."

"Why here?"

"Blade asked me to."

"But to do what?"

"I don't know. She said I'd know when I got here."

She suddenly seems deep in thought and shakes her head slowly.

"What is it?" I ask.

"Just what we were talkin' about earlier," she says. "The trust you two have. I want that. And if I'm honest . . . I'd like it with you."

35

Maddie Marie's is an old hunting lodge on the edge of Tate's Hell.

Tate's Hell is over 200,000 acres of dense flatwood and floodplain forest, wet prairie, seepage slope, and impenetrable swamp.

Legend has it that back in the 1870s a homesteader named Cebe Tate ventured into the woods with his hunting dogs to kill a panther that had attacked his livestock. Getting separated from his dogs and becoming lost for several days, when he finally merged from the wicked woods he uttered these haunting words, "My name is Cebe Tate, and I just came from Hell."

As soon as I pull onto the property, Maddie opens the front door of the lodge and comes out to meet me, which means though I didn't spot them, there are security cameras hidden about.

Leaving Lexi in the car, I get out to greet Maddie.

"Burke," she says.

"How are you, Maddie?"

"Better than I deserve to be."

Maddie is a harsh, weathered woman of indeterminate age. She's an ex-heroin addict and sex worker who has served time in both prison and psych hospitals. She now spends her days working with the mentally ill and drug addicted in a one-on-one manner that can only be described as fully immersive.

She is thick and muscular, her dark skin wrinkled and sun-damaged, her coarse brown hair wild and wooly.

"Blade get arrested?" she asks.

I nod.

"Figured . . . when you showed up."

Behind her the old dilapidated white clapboard lodge leans to the left and appears not to be long for this world, as if at any moment it may slip into the swamp and sink into oblivion.

"What's going on?" I ask.

"I don't know exactly what she wants me to do," she says, "but there's nothing I can do. She knows that. She knew that when we made this little arrangement."

"What arrangement?" I ask. "Is . . . is Chrissy Violet a patient here?"

"Who is or isn't a patient here is confidential," she says, "but if she were . . . if Blade brought me someone who needed to be put down but instead of killing her brought her to me for . . . treatment . . . then she knew that she couldn't come out or have any contact with anyone from the outside world until that treatment is completed."

So instead of killing Chrissy, Blade brought her here for healing. It was the best possible thing she could've done for her —and had the added benefit of seeing if Cindi Rush was worthy of her trust and devotion.

"Which is how long?"

She shakes her head. "Takes as long as it takes. But ain't ever quick."

"I know your . . . approach works," I say.

She shakes her head. "Only some of the time—just a lot more than any other programs out there."

"And I don't want to do anything to jeopardize Chrissy's best chance at unfucking her head."

"I wouldn't let you," she says. "No matter what I owe you."

"But . . . I can't just leave Blade in jail."

"She knew what she was signing up for when she brought her," I say.

"Well, it wasn't sitting in jail for something she didn't do."

"Nothin' I can do for you, Burke. I'm sorry. Now you go on back to civilization and forget all about this little conversation."

36

———————

"She never ceases to amaze," Ben says.

"Never," I say.

We are in my office waiting for Kirkland.

"Thought for sure she had killed her," he says.

"Pretty fair assumption given what Violet had done to her."

"But," he says, "she tried to help her."

"Yes, she did," I say, and I feel my eyes moistening.

To our surprise, when Kirkland shows up he has Blade with him.

I jump up and run over and hug the shit out of her.

"I ain't even been gone a day," she says.

"That was for what you did," I said. "You ain't been gone long enough for me to miss you yet."

"I've got respect for you kids," Kirkland says. "I really do. I appreciate what y'all've done with your lives and what it took for you to get to where you are. I'm not tryin' to be an asshole and if there's anything I can do to help you I will, but . . . I can't let murder go unpunished. I just can't. No matter what the person did."

"She didn't murder anyone," Ben says.

"So you said," Kirkland says. "But I can't just take your word for it. I have to have proof."

Ben says, "Luc, why don't you tell him where you went this morning and what you found?"

I do.

"I hope that's the case," Kirkland says. "I really do."

Blade says, "It is. Don't get me wrong . . . I wanted to pop her. I did. But . . . Maddie Marie popped into my head and I's like . . . if anyone can turn this bitch around it's her. 'Cause even after what she had done to us . . . if I took her off the board it'd be an execution, a . . . Killin' somebody in cold blood is . . . There may come a day when somebody does something that 'causes me to have to do something like that, but . . . that day ain't arrived just yet."

"I can't just take your word for it that she's alive and in that home," Kirkland says.

"I know," I say. "And I don't expect you to, but . . . Maddie's program doesn't allow for any contact whatsoever between her patients and the outside world."

"She might have to make an exception this once."

"She won't," Blade says.

"She might," Kirkland says. "For a court order."

"You do something like that and everything I've done is in vain," Blade says.

"Well, I don't know what you want me to do," he says, "but I have to have proof and I can't have an innocent woman sitting in a jail cell. I just can't."

Ben says, "Maybe we can figure out a compromise."

"It's not in Maddie's vocabulary," Blade says. "And if you force her into something it'll not only derail Chrissy's treatment but burn every bridge we have with her. And given the sick pricks we work with . . . we gonna need her services again in the future."

"Then what?" Kirkland says. "What would you have me do? Tell you what . . . I'll give you a couple of days. Either figure something out or I'm showing up there with a court order. I can't just take your word for it, and I can't have an innocent woman sitting in our jail."

"Thank you," I say. "I appreciate that. We'll figure something out."

When they are gone I call Heather.

"Hey," she says.

"Hey."

There's an awkward moment where neither of us says anything.

"I'm calling to say I'm sorry again," I say.

"How many times you planning on apologizing?"

"I feel so embarrassed and ashamed."

"I understand but you've got to let it go and—"

"Did I scare you?" I ask.

"No, but I'm not a coatrack."

"I would never hurt you," I say.

"You were defending and protecting me," she says. "I never for one moment felt unsafe."

"Good."

"I hate that you carry that much rage around with you," she says.

"I'm sorry you were anywhere near it when it came pouring out."

"Are you getting help?"

"Counseling *and* a support group," I say. "Can't you tell?"

"Can you even imagine what your life would be like without that inside of you?"

"Not really," I say.

Another moment of silence passes between us, but this one lacks the awkwardness of the first.

"Well," I say, "I just wanted to say how sorry I am."

"Why don't you tell me in person sometime," she says.

"Didn't figure you'd ever want to be around me again."

"You kidding? I have this nearly overwhelming urge to hold and console you."

37

"I's on my way to kill her," Blade is saying. "Had every intention. Then I began to think about what you said."

I think about pleading with her not to do it. I was incapacitated at the time and pleading was about all I could do, but for her sake I begged her.

"I really thought you had killed her," I say.

We are in my car headed back to Apalach to attempt to reason with Maddie one more time before the cops knock her door down.

Blade has bonded out, bail only becoming an option when Kirkland made the DA aware of his belief that Chrissy Violet is still alive.

"I look at how your charges hang over you," she says. "How that effects you. And that was just for a little aggravated battery. And I's like this crazy bitch ain't worth that. And if she's crazy as I'm thinkin' she is . . . she'll probably make another run at me and I can put her down and it be self-defense. So . . . I came close to callin' the cops and turning her in, but . . . I had already broken into the office and stolen the surveillance system . . . and then out of nowhere . . . I thought of Maddie's program. I's like maybe she can cure the bitch. I had already dropped Rush off. I started to call you to go with me, but then I'd like . . . I'm really, really into this girl, but I can tell she's weak. See what happens if she think I killed Violet. And sure enough . . . only lasted a few weeks before betraying the fuck out of me."

"Wonder how many people would've passed that test?"

"You sayin' it wasn't fair?"

"I'm sayin' I wonder how many people would pass it," I say. "I'm sayin' we have trust issues like a mofo. I'm sayin' it was a hell of a test for such a new relationship."

"Her crazy ex dealt the play, not me."

I don't say anything.

"What, you don't think she did?"

"She dealt the first hand for sure," I say. "But you raised the fuck out of it."

"Sure as shit not gonna fold," she says. "That's not in my nature."

"I know."

She nods to herself. "And now I know about Rush."

It was an unfair test and Blade should give her another chance, but I know she never will. And yet . . . maybe I'm wrong. She certainly surprised me with what she did with Chrissy Violet. Maybe she'll surprise me when it comes to Rush too, but I doubt it. And what's even more concerning is I doubt anyone will ever pass any of her tests.

As we near Apalach she says, "You got any kind of a plan? 'Cause Maddie don't play. She gladly let my ass sit in jail 'stead of compromising her program."

"Not sayin' it's gonna work, but I have a plan. And it involves today's paper."

I pull into a convenience store, jump out and buy a copy of today's *Tallahassee Democrat*.

When I get back in the car, Blade says, "I seriously doubt the bitch can read. So . . . don't know how this gonna help."

A few minutes later when we pull up to Maddie's place, she is out the door and arriving at our car by the time we're getting out.

"Y'all're as hardheaded as I am," she says.

"Nobody that hardheaded," Blade says.

"Don't know why y'all are back," Maddie says. "Nothin's changed."

"We have to have proof that Chrissy is alive," I say.

"You'll just have to take my word for it."

"Thing is," I say. "The cop in charge of the case can't let Blade sit in jail if there's even a possibility that Chrissy is alive, so if we don't figure something out he'll be showing up here with a court order to come into your place and verify she's here."

She starts to say something but I keep going.

"But I think I have a solution that will be the least intrusive on Chrissy and the work you're doing."

"I'm listening."

"You take my phone in there and shoot a short video of Chrissy confirming she's alive and well and here of her own volition while holding today's paper to verify the date. It'll take a few seconds and we won't be back and neither will the cops."

"Don't let it be said that I'm not a reasonable person," she says. "But know y'all are burnin' a bridge here."

"*Shee-it*," Blade says. "That's what we doin' all this *not* to do."

38

Tip Ripper operates the only Raven LuRue fan site in the area. He hired Ward Forester to find Hillary York. And we're pretty sure he's the goth guy who upset Brook the night of her bachelorette party.

When he's not worshiping Raven and sharing in detail how he'd like to torture, rape, and murder Hillary York, he's out on the town gothing it up. When he's not doing any of those things he's hawking comic books and fantasy games at The Dungeon, a dark comic book and gaming shop in a house I'm pretty sure is not zoned commercial near the old airport.

He's about as pale as I've ever seen a living human being be, with long, straight, dyed black hair, a variety of facial piercings, and reptilian contacts that make interacting with him like talking to a snake. He's tall and extremely thin, his black eyeliner and nail polish matching his hair.

Blade and I have come to have a little chat with him. The proof of life video of Chrissy Violet we delivered to Bob Kirkland was enough to keep her out of jail for now, but he wants to see Chrissy in person as soon as she has completed Maddie's program.

We find him in what was once the living room and is now the comic book part of the shop shelving serial killer graphic novels. Down the hallway in what used to be bedrooms, pale pimply-faced virgins are pretending to be someone—anyone—other than who they are.

"You ever met Raven?" I ask.

He turns and looks at a personalized and signed poster hanging behind the checkout counter.

The poster and the accompanying photo of Raven and Tip are of the pay-for-play fan cult VIP variety. No doubt Tip paid big bucks, along with several other fans, for a few moments with his idol before an overpriced show.

"Is that him playing?" I ask, nodding toward the agitating noise coming from the speakers hanging from the ceiling.

"It's all we play here."

Outside, The Dungeon looks like a small, old house in disrepair. Inside, it looks like a medieval dungeon set from a bad B movie was used to decorate a comic book shop. The only thing going for it is that it's dim and has very few patrons—at least out here where we are.

"Why'd you hire Ward Forester to find Hillary York?"

Ward didn't come out and tell us Tip had hired him, but he he didn't deny it either.

"Evil bitch needs to be punished."

He just confirmed for us what Ward couldn't because of client confidentiality.

"For what?" I ask.

"Lying about Raven."

We have no idea what if anything Tip knows about Hillary York or Brooklyn Hill, so we're going to try to thread the needle of getting information from him without giving him any.

Blade says, "So you want to do to her what she said Raven did to her—and worse—because he *didn't* do it?"

"What?" he asks, confused.

"Just some actual irony for Alanis Morissette if she ever decides to do a rewrite."

When he licks his lips I can see he's had his tongue cut in two to make it forked and serpent like.

"Let me ask you something," I say. "If everything Ms. York alleged were true, would it lose Raven a single fan?"

He shakes his head.

"*Shee-it*," Blade says. "Probably earn him some new ones."

Tip smiles sickly, licks his lips lasciviously and nods.

"So why do you want to punish her?"

"His record label dropped him," he says. "He lost all his film and TV roles. His tour. Everything."

"Robbing the world of all that amazing art," Blade says. "Bitch does need to be punished."

"Any idea where she is?" I ask.

"If I knew that I wouldn't've hired a PI to find her."

"Why hire a Panama City PI?" I ask.

"And why him instead of us?" Blade asks.

"Nothin' personal," he says. "I just saw his ad and called him."

"But why hire a local investigator?" I ask. "Do you think she's here?"

"In *Panama City*?" he asks, his voice rising in surprise. "Fuck no. He said he works all over the world and can find her no matter where she is. Did I get taken for a ride?"

"No," I say.

"He said he's the best."

"Well," Blade says, "he lied to you about that."

"Should I fire him and hire y'all?"

"Depends on if you want to find her or not," Blade says.

"What're you going to do when you find her?" I ask.

"Let Raven know where she is."

"And?"

"And that's it."

Blade says, "What about all the torturing, raping, and murdering?"

"Metaphors," he says. "Fantasies. Not meant to be taken literal."

He shakes his head and blinks his eyes as if something has just occurred to him and he turns to Blade. "Didn't you just get arrested for killin' a crazy bitch?"

"I did, but the charges were just metaphorical."

"I should hire y'all," he says. "Other dude's too old and straight edge anyway."

"What do you want us to do when we find her?" I ask.

"Just let me know where she is."

"Any ideas where she might be?"

He shakes his head. "After she spewed out all her lies about Raven she just vanished."

"Sure *he* didn't kill her?" Blade says.

"There're a lot of people who think so."

"But not you?"

"I don't know. But I'm dyin' to know. I feel like . . . if I knew .. . for sure . . . it'd bring us closer together."

I want to ask him about his presence at Ms. Newby's on the night Brook went missing but can't take the chance he'll connect Brook and Hillary if he doesn't already know. We've checked on Raven's whereabouts during that time and he was in Germany, so unless he hired someone to do it for him he's not involved.

I decide the best way to find out everything he knows and reveal nothing that we know to him is to let him hire us.

"You serious about wanting to hire us?" I ask.

He shrugs.

"Here's the thing," I say. "We not only say we're the best, we back it up. When you hire us . . . you don't pay a single cent unless we do what you hire us to do. That's how confident we are that we can deliver."

"Shit yeah," he says.

"But when we do deliver," Blade says. "You pay up."

"How much?"

"Depends," I say. "What exactly do you want us to do?"

"Just find out what happened to the girl and where she is," he says. "That's it."

"That's it?" I say. "Nothing else? No torturing. No raping. No killing."

"I just want to know what happened to her and where she is."

"And what info are you providing for us?"

"Tons," he says. "I've been researching this from day one. Likely theories. Sightings."

"Where has she been sighted?" I ask. "Where do you think she is?"

"Fort Wayne, Indiana, and Toronto, Ontario, Canada."

"You give us everything you got," I say. "Tell us everything you know. That way we don't waste time doing work you've already done. And we'll find her for two grand."

"Plus expenses," Blade says. "We got to fly to fuckin' Canada, that's on you."

"You believe him?" Blade asks.

I shrug.

Tip Ripper hired us for no money down and gave us his files and told us which Reddit theories are most likely real.

If he was honest, he knows next to nothing—and nothing at all that a cursory glance at the online info wouldn't tell you.

"Be a big ass coincidence for him to be at the club where she was and hire a PI to find her if he didn't know she was here."

"True," she says. "Also true—no one was ever overheard saying, 'Golly Gee, Doris, can't get anything passed that genius, Tip, now can you?'"

"*Doris?*" I say. "*Golly Gee?*"

"Least we'll soon know if he was at Newby's that night," she says.

We told him we needed to snap a pic of him—something we did with all our clients. And he both believed us and let us. A picture we plan to pass around to the bridesmaids to see if any of them recognize him from the night Brook disappeared.

"Think we should text it to them or do it in person?" I ask.

"If we text it it needs to be to each one individually, not a group text. Want their reactions to be their own and not in relation to each other."

I nod.

"But face to face give us a chance to see how they react and fire off some follow up questions at them."

"True."

"Probably gonna have to do some by phone even if we try to meet with as many of them as we can."

"Let's start with Olivia since she's the one who told us about him"

She nods. "Hell, she may be the only one who noticed him."

I pull out my phone and call Olivia.

She is finishing up a workout at a gym in the old mall and says she's willing to talk with us there.

Built in the 70s, the Panama City Mall went through many changes and iterations over the decades, and even though it was in decline, it was still surviving when the Cat 5 super storm Hurricane Michael hit it back in October of 2018. It has been closed ever since. However a few places attached to the mall actually survived—three anchor department stores and Planet Fitness.

We meet with Olivia near her car in the mostly empty lot outside of Planet Fitness.

She is wearing stylish workout attire, guzzling water from a purple Planet Fitness water bottle, and her hair is damp.

"Thanks for meeting with us," I say. "Won't take but a second."

"No problem."

I open my phone, flip to the photo of Tip Ripper, and hold it up to her.

She studies it.

"That him?" I ask.

"From Newby's that night? I think so. But I want to be sure. I know how often eyewitnesses get it wrong."

She takes my phone and looks at the picture with even more focus and intensity.

It's dark and only some of the lights in the pocked and oil-stained parking lot are working. Before us, people committed to their conditioning can be seen jogging and working out on the purple and gold machines in the brightly lit gym while behind us a steady stream of vehicles breeze by out on MLK.

"Horrible thing for a black woman to say," Olivia says, "but they all look alike."

"Goths?" I ask.

"Yeah."

"Sort of the point," Blade says. "It's a uniform."

"I can't be positive, but I believe it's him."

"Do you know if any of the other bridesmaids got a look at him?" I ask.

"Only one I know for sure is Zoey."

"Thanks."

After we make sure Olivia gets in her car safely, we get back in ours and call Zoey Wanamaker.

A short while later we're meeting with her near her car in the parking lot in front of Publix where she had been shopping.

"I like shopping at night when there's not as many people around," she says.

"I like doin' everything when there ain't as many people around," Blade says.

"Just one of the many things you two have in common," I say.

Blade laughs but Zoey doesn't react.

As if she hasn't changed since her school day ended over five hours ago, Zoey is wearing a matronly cotton dress with ABCs and chalkboards and apples and students and desks. The material of the dress is thin, its construction poor, and it is unflattering to her soft, slightly chubby frame.

"I really need to be going," she says. "Still have to work on some lesson plans and crafts for tomorrow. What can I do for you?"

Her tone has changed. My comment obviously offended her.

"Do you remember seeing a goth at Newby's the night Brook disappeared?"

She nods.

"Try to remember him," I say. "Close your eyes and picture him in your mind with as much detail as you can."

She closes her eyes and seems to be attempting to do what I've asked.

I hold my phone up in front of her, the photo of Tip filling the screen.

"Now, open your eyes and tell me if this is the guy."

She opens her eyes and immediately starts nodding. "That's him. Who is he? Did he take Brook? That's him. What is wrong with people? Look at him. I don't understand the world we live in anymore. What did he do to her? *Why* did he do it?"

Before I can respond, a van pulls around and passes, and as I glance over at the two older women in it everything falls into place.

"*Oh, shit,*" Blade says, staring at me. "You just figured it out, didn't you?"

"Did you?" Zoey says. "Was it him? How'd he do it? Tell me. I need to know. Please. Where is Brook? Who killed her?"

40

"Solved the crime in the fuckin' Publix parking lot," Blade is saying.

"I'm gonna drive and think," I say.

"That your way of sayin' *Keep your big mouth shut, Blade*?"

"Yeah."

"I can do that," she says, "but you gotta give me somethin'."

"Those two women in the van just then," I say. "They made me think of the two that Todd Johns saw when he dropped the bridesmaids off at the hotel that night."

"Okay?"

"Brooks had run before," I say. "What if something made her run again?"

"Okay?"

"What if the two women in the van that night were part of one of those domestic abuse programs? What if they were there to pick her up and take her away?"

"It's possible," she says. "But Brook wasn't there, so . . . they couldn't've gotten her. Are you sayin' Liam was abusing her?"

"No."

"Then what?"

"Let me think everything through and see if there are any holes in my theory."

"Think I already poked a big one in it but okay."

I drive and think while Blade messes around on her phone.

I go over everything I know about the night Brook went missing again—the phone call, the change, the bachelor party, the goth, the bridesmaids, the search dogs, Chase, Liam, Harley Chandler, Raven LuRue, the two women in the van, the appearances versus the reality, the going back to Jungle Jim's, the security team, especially Gainer, the surveillance footage, the bathroom, the last dance, and I think it all fits.

When I pull up in front of Harper's gallery, Blade looks at me with raised eyebrows and says, *"Oh. Hell. Yeah."*

41

Harper doesn't want to unlock the door for us, but we insist, and when she sees the look on my face, her entire countenance falls.

"I know," I say.

The truth is I don't *know* anything. I only suspect. I only have a theory. But there's no need for her to know that.

She backs into her gallery and collapses into the small wooden bench intended for sitting and studying the art on the walls—though I can't imagine anyone ever has.

"You're a good friend," I say.

Blade glances at me to see if I'm being sarcastic, but I'm not.

"You were the only one who knew her secret," I say. "The only one she really trusted. So of course she turned to you when she decided to do a runner again."

She nods.

"It started with the phone call from Liam," I say. "None of this was planned before then, was it?"

She shakes her head.

"He scared her, didn't he?"

"Liam's a good guy," she says. "He really is. He's safe. He's dependable. But he's . . . He was just enough overprotective . . . over . . . bearing . . . that she felt controlled. Felt . . . Had flashbacks to Raven and . . . freaked out. When he asked her not to go that night . . . she started feeling it, but when he said he was going to follow us . . . that was it. He only wanted her safe. He was being the protector he is, but she . . . flipped. Fight or flight kicked in again and she decided to fly. I tried to talk her out of it, to reason with her, but . . . nothing I said did any good. I couldn't get through. So I decided to help her."

"It helps that y'all look alike," I say. "But the TEAM BRIDE sunglasses and her not talking made the biggest different."

"How did you . . . How do you know?"

"Yeah," Blade says. "Spill."

"She called a domestic abuse hotline and arranged to be picked up later that night," I say. "I bet she had their number programmed in her phone and had an exit strategy in place so she would walk out of her life at a moment's notice."

"That's what Raven did to her," Harper says.

"So the two lezzes in the van were there to take her away," Blade says, "but she wasn't there."

"Yes, she was," I say. "Harper wasn't there, but Brook was. They swapped places. Went into the bathroom before the last dance and exchanged outfits. The video footage shows Harper coming out but not Brook. But it wasn't Harper. It was Brook in Harper's clothes. She kept on her TEAM BRIDE sunglasses and pretended to sleep on the way back to the hotel so she didn't have to speak. It's why the scent dog tracked her walking out the front door and down the escalator. All the while Harper is hiding in Jungle Jim's. That's why you didn't know there were two cops on the landing instead of one like when y'all arrived. Brook gets back to the hotel and pretends to crash but really sneaks out into the night and gets in the van with the domestic abuse volunteers. And she's gone. I suspect she just used them for the first part of her getaway. Unlike most of the women they help she has the resources and the knowhow to vanish on her own. You hide out in Jungle Jim's all night. Then the next morning scare the shit out of Gainer because he wasn't expecting anyone. And he wasn't expecting anyone because he unlocked the door when he came in and locked it back behind him. No one should've been inside, but you were because you were already in there. The first time the surveillance footage shows you is when you approach Gainer. It doesn't show you arrive or knock on the door or be let in because you were already in."

"I feel so bad for Liam," she says. "The other bridesmaids too. Some of them—Zoey. Olivia. The ones who really care. They're all innocent and have no idea what really happened. But I had to help her, had to do what I could to make her feel safe. It was such an overreaction, but . . . her PTSD was so severe and . . . seeing the goth guy at the club just reinforced all her fears and flight reflexes."

"Where she now?" Blade asks.

Harper shakes her head. "No idea. Haven't spoken to her since that night and I knew when I agreed to help her I'd never hear from her again. She's gone. No one will ever find her."

"Challenge accepted," Blade says.

"Why would you want to find her?" Harper asks. "She's free. She's safe. She doesn't want to be found."

"We can't know that for sure without seeing her," I say. "Talking to her. We've got to know for sure that Raven or one of his minions didn't find her. They're still looking."

"You'll never find her," Harper says. "We'll never know where she is or what she's doing. Whatever her fate was . . . we'll never know. That's not easy to live with but I've learned to. And you will too . . . over time."

"Finding people is what we do," Blade says.

"Not like this," she says. "Not this person. She's even more gone than your sister."

"Bitch just got personal," Blade says. "Sure as shit findin' her white ass now."

42

———————

"**G**otta hand it to you," Blade says. "That was some impressive shit back there."

We are in my car headed back to the office for her to get hers.

"I really thought Chase's creepy ass was gonna turn out to be involved," she adds.

I nod. "No tellin' what all he's involved in—just not this. Wouldn't be surprised if we encounter him again some day."

"No way I could'a put all that shit together," she says, "connected all those dots. You better than me at this."

"At what?"

"Detecting," she says.

I shake my head. "Not true. There's a lot more to what we do than drawing some inferences and connecting some dots. We're good at different aspects of this work, and our gifts and abilities compliment each other."

"Not sayin' they don't," she says. "And you know I know my value. But what you did tonight was impressive. And I'm tellin' you so shut the fuck up and take the compliment. You've always been good at figuring out the puzzle part."

"Which most cases we take on don't even have."

"Again, not the point. I'm sayin' you're good at deductive reasoning and shit, and what you did tonight . . . Wasn't just me who couldn't do that shit. No one else could either. Not the cops. Not the DA. Not the lawyers. Not the bitches who were there and saw it happen. And not the thousands of internet sleuths. Only you."

"Well, thank you," I say. "I appreciate you . . . Thank you. Not sure it gets us any closer to finding Brook."

"You think Harper was right?" she asks.

"About?"

"That she'll never be found."

I shrug. "Guess we gonna find out."

She nods. "Guess so."

"If we could know for sure she's okay and wants to be where she is . . ."

"But we can't."

"Maybe we shouldn't . . . even look for her," I say. "She obviously doesn't want to be found."

"We can't just take Harper's word for everything," she says. "'Sides, even if it was her decision to do a runner, who's to say somebody didn't snatch her before she was able to or even after she got to where she was going?"

She's right. There's no way for us to know. I have no interest in finding anyone who doesn't want to be found, but without knowing for sure that she doesn't it's hard justifying doing nothing.

"Probably won't be able to find her ass anyway," she says.

"True. It won't be easy. And it may not be possible."

"We gonna need you to put that big brain of yours to work on figuring out where we even start."

"I's thinkin' since I figured out what happened the night of Brook's disappearance you'd handle this one. You the brains of this outfit," she says. "I the brawn—and the beauty. Stay in your lane, bruh, and do your damn job."

43

―――――

When I stop by Dave's Corner Pub to pay for the damages I inflicted on the joint, the bartender, an older white woman with huge hair, told me that Heather Harrison had already taken care of it.

I step out to the parking lot and call her.

Not wanting to get back in the car yet and not having anywhere to be, I walk down the sidewalk next to 15th Street—east toward downtown.

A brilliant orangish moon hangs low in the inky night sky, the bottom of its full, orb-like figure seeming to touch the tips of the tree line along the horizon. The night is cool, the traffic relatively light, and it feels fantastic to walk.

"I got more money than people to spend it on these days," she says. "Just wanted to do a little something for you."

"That wasn't little," I say.

"It really was."

"I'm overwhelmed," I say. "I . . . I'm so grateful. Thank you."

"My pleasure," she says. "Truly."

"I—"

"And look," she adds, "there are no strings attached. It's a gift. You don't owe me anything, not indebted to me in any way. I'm still deeply indebted to you. And to Blade. But that's not why I did it. I just wanted to do something nice for you."

"Well, it's one of the nicest things anyone has ever done for me," I say.

She doesn't say anything but I can tell in the change of her breathing and bearing she finds that sad.

"If I promise not to break anything, would you like to meet for a drink somewhere?" I ask.

"I'd love to, but I can' t tonight," she says.

"I'd understand if you never want to chance that happening again," I say.

"It's not that," she says. "I swear. Ask me another time. Please."

"I will."

"Have a good rest of your night and take good care of yourself," she says and hops off the call.

As I turn around and head west back toward Dave's, I can't help but think something other than what was said was going on. Somewhere in the course of the conversation something had changed and I had no idea why. I didn't even know what the change was exactly, but—

My phone vibrates and I pull it out of my pocket hoping it's Heather calling back.

It's Ashlynn.

"Hey," I say.

"Where are you?" she asks, her voice tense and tight.

"15th near Dave's. What's wrong?"

"I'm at your place with Alana. Please get here as fast as you can."

44

———

I drive as fast as I can to my place.

Ashlynn has a key and she and Alana are already inside, but she has the deadbolt on and I'm unable to get in.

I tap on the door gently and say, "Ashlynn, it's me."

I can hear the deadbolt being disengaged. She opens the door, shielding herself behind it, and closes it back as soon as I'm inside. She then re-engages the deadbolt.

"What is it?" I ask. "What's wrong?"

She and Alana appear fine. No obvious wounds.

Alana runs up to hug me and I pick her up and hug her and look back at Ashlynn. "What's going on?"

"I'm okay. We're okay. I'm just . . . I got s-c-a-r-e-d." She spells out the word so as not to alarm Alana any more than she already is.

I look at Alana. "How are you doing today, pretty girl?"

"Can we go get some ice cream?"

"Sure," I say. "Just give me a few minutes to talk to mommy. Can you play with your—"

"I want to watch your phone."

"Sure," I say. "That's a great idea."

I take her over to the couch, find her a non-scary Sonic the Hedgehog video, and give her my phone.

I then meet Ashlynn in the kitchen where she is knocking back a shot of bourbon.

"Tell me what's going on," I say, my voice low and soft.

"Dimitri found out we're related," she says. "Fired me."

"I wanted you out of there anyway," I say. "You can work somewhere else."

"It's not that—I mean, I didn't want to lose my job, but . . . I can get work . . . He . . . He said he was going to kill you, but before he did he'd make me and Alana suffer. Said he was going to disfigure us with a knife like the one Blade used on him. Said he was going to mark us as his property. Said that's what we'd be as soon as you and Blade were in the ground. He said . . . he was going to . . . pimp us both out. Both of us. I could tell he meant it, that the idea of it made him . . . gave him pleasure."

"I'm so sorry," I say. "Did he do anything to you today?"

She shakes her head. "Told me he'd let me think about it for a while first. He's a . . . a . . . a legit sociopath. You could tell he had no . . . that he felt nothing but excitement about telling me all the ways he would torture and violate both me and Alana and that he would enjoy every moment of it when he finally does it."

"I'm so, so sorry," I say. "But we're not going to let anything happen to you or Alana. Y'all can move in here. Don't worry about work or anything else. We'll have protection with y'all at all times. We'll keep y'all safe until this is over."

"It's not going to be over," she says. "Not until we're dead or he is."

45

When I open the door for Blade she's holding a shotgun in one hand and a backpack in the other.

"Brought some firepower since your parolee ass doesn't have any."

She steps in and I close and lock the door.

"Whattcha gonna do when Dimitri and Bogdan come?" she asks. "Glare? Growl? Use harsh language?"

It's later the same night. Ashlynn and Alana are asleep in my bed, the door closed and locked.

"Thanks for coming over," I say.

"Brawn and beauty," she says.

"No doubt."

While she settles in, I make a few calls.

I let Ben know what's going on, and he agrees to implement more security measures around the office—including keeping the exterior door locked and only allowing clients in once their identity has been verified.

Next I call Lexi.

"Hey," she says, her voice sleepy, her mouth dry. "Please tell me this is a booty call."

"I wish," I say. "But I'm afraid it's the opposite."

I quickly tell her what's happening. "I don't think he'll come after you, but I wanted you to be more careful in general and around me in particular."

"Let me know what I can do," she says. "I can sit watch with them. I'm armed and legal. Something happens I can say I was there for your monthly visit and intervened when this crazy Russian tried to kill a young mother and her child."

"Thanks."

When I end the call with her I call Pete.

After I tell him what's going on he says, "We've got to do something about this Russian problem."

"Let me know if you come up with anything," I say. "Be nice to have some official leverage to use against him."

"I'll work on finding some. Meantime, just let me know when you need me to stay with Ashlynn and Alana—or better yet when you want them to stay with me."

"Thanks."

Though it's late by the time I get around to calling Heather Harrison it's obvious she's wide awake.

"I'm so glad you called," she says.

"You are?" I say. "I got the feeling earlier you didn't want to—"

"Sorry about that. I was being . . . It was . . . The reason I said no to your kind invitation is I didn't want you doing it out of obligation or because you felt you had to since I had paid Dave's for the damage. That was all. It was stupid. I've regretted it ever since. I'm sorry."

"I'm so grateful for what you did," I say, "but it wasn't tryin' to pay you back."

"I'm glad. I just don't want you thinking you owe me anything," she says. "And I didn't do it because I owe you so much. I did it because I wanted to. No other reason. No strings. No obligations."

"Same goes for when I ask you to get a drink."

"Got it."

"Glad we got that cleared up," I say, "but I'm calling for another reason. I don't think it will have any effect on you, but I wanted you to be aware and ask you to take extra precautions—especially around me."

"What is it?"

I tell her.

"Oh, Luc, I'm so sorry. Let me know what I can do to help. It was very sweet of you to warn me. Thank you. And, hey, the condo is empty. You're more than welcome to put Ashlynn and Alana in it. They have absolutely no connection to it and no one would ever guess they were there."

"Thank you," I say. "I really appreciate that. That's a much more secure and safe location than my place and I may just take you up on that."

When I end the call I join Blade on the couch.

"'Sup?" she says.

"Heather offered her condo as a safe house for Ashlynn and Alana."

She nods. "That'd be a lot, lot better than here. We should do that. What was that other shit? The obligation stuff."

I tell her about Heather paying for the damages at Dave's and what happened when I asked her out afterwards.

"Sugar mama," she says. "Wow. I thought she was just your surrogate mama sexually, but damn you gettin' the full mama monty."

"I've about reached the limit of the mom comments," I say.

"Oh, you have?" she says, her voice growing soft and tender. "I'm sorry. 'Cause there's a ton more to come."

I laugh.

"Nah, for real man, how are you less fucked up than me?"

Something in her changes. It's a rare moment of seriousness.

"Clearly I'm not," I say.

"I mean . . . how the hell that happen?"

"It didn't," I say. "Not by any objective measurement. Did you see what I did to Dave's? What're you even—"

"You got two things goin'," she says.

"You mean Lexi and Heather?"

"I can't even have one."

She's rarely ever this vulnerable. It's jolting.

"One's my probation officer and one's almost old enough to be the mom I never had," I say. "And I'm bouncing between them like a—"

"The fuck's wrong with me?" she says. "Testing Rush like that? Settin' her up to fail so I can push her away."

Regardless of who is more fucked up, we're both damaged —lost and alone in the world, motherless, fatherless, full of fear and rage, suffering from PTSD, childhood trauma, and overachieving abandonment issues.

"I'm like the runaway bride we lookin' for," she says. "Doin' a runner for no reason. Don't think I'll ever be able to have . . . something . . . *anything*." She shakes her head. "Can't let anybody in."

"You can change that," I say.

"I don't think I can."

"You could call Rush right now and tell her—"

"No, I couldn't."

"I could call her for you."

"I could shoot you in the face with my shotgun."

46

"**S**omethin's got to be done," Clyde is saying.

"I'm open to suggestions," I say.

It's the next morning. Blade is at my place with Ashlynn and Alana. I'm in our office with Clyde.

"Everything I'm thinkin' ends with one less Russian in the world—two if his fat lackey gets in the way."

Though not as tall as Bogdan, Clyde is every bit as big as him, and it's funny to hear him refer to Bogdan as fat.

"What a wonderful world it would be," I sing.

He shakes his head and feigns embarrassment for me.

"You heard anything about how his transition to power's going?" I ask.

"Hear it ain't good," he says. "Nobody likes him. Nobody respects him. Some of them fear him but not just 'cause he's dangerous but because he's crazy and unpredictable too."

"Any chance some other member of the Russian mob will take him out?"

He nods. "They's a good chance, but probably won't be right away . . . and how much damage can he do before that happens?"

"I actually know the answer to that one," I say. "A lot."

He nods as he frowns and lets out a long, slow, worldweary sigh.

"Speaking of bad guys who do damage," I say, "Logan's been quiet lately. What's going on with him?"

He shakes his head and rolls his eyes. "He's on safari."

"Safari?"

"Safari," he says. "In fuckin' South Africa. Dropped ten grand to try and kill a cape buffalo."

"He seems like the type," I say.

"So I got some time on my hands," he says. "Lookin' for somethin' to do. Figured I might start a little side hustle in extermination. Deal with this infestation of Russian roaches. My grandma always said idle hands are the devil's workshop."

"Let me know what I can do to help. I like supporting black-owned businesses."

"Will do, but just concentrate on keepin' that little girl safe. Things may get worse before they get better."

47

———

"**I**s it true?" Zoey asks.

"Is what true?" I ask.

She, Liam, and Ben have just come into my office.

As if a uniform, she's wearing the same school-themed dress as before.

It's a couple of hours later. I've been trying to figure out a way to find Brook. Zoey and Ben take the two client chairs. Liam leans against the wall.

"That she just ran away," she says. "From a good man like him. And Harper helped her."

"What're you—"

"Harper told me," Liam says. "Said it would all be coming out soon and she wanted me to hear it from her."

Ben looks at me and shakes his head.

"It wasn't going to come out," I say. "Not from us. I was going to tell Ben but haven't even had a chance to do that yet."

"So you were going to tell me," he says.

"Of course."

"Well, that's you off the hook," Ben says to Liam. "No way the DA will charge you now."

"How do we find her?" Liam says. "She just got scared. Because of what that evil son of a bitch did to her. She wasn't thinking straight. She ... And now she's out there all alone. I've got to find her and convince her that she's safe with me."

Zoey says, "Harper said she'd never be found."

Something in the way she says it makes me think that would be just fine with her.

"If what she's sayin' is true," Ben says, "it's hard to see how she will be."

"Still can't believe she did this to us," Zoey says. "To Liam."

"Can you find her?" Liam asks me. "I'll pay whatever it costs." He turns to Ben. "If I'm not going on trial I can use that money to find Brook, right?"

Ben nods and I can see in his eyes he's calculating how much money he just lost.

"You're already paying us to find her," I say. "We're still looking."

"But with more money we can get more resources—and if she's as well hidden as y'all say sounds like we're going to need them."

Harper appears at the door, followed by Olivia and Willow.

Standing so close together contrasts Olivia's olive skin and Willow's red-tinted, freckle-flecked paleness. Both women are attractive, like every other member of the bridesmaids, and I wonder if Brook had any unattractive friends. Zoey comes the closest to fitting that bill because of her extra weight, awkwardness, and occasional condescending obnoxiousness.

"Everyone knows now?" I say as they step inside. "This feels like a fuckin' *Friends* episode."

Olivia says, "You know how fast gossip spreads through a group like this? Poppy and Annabeth don't know, but they're not really part of the group."

Zoey stands up and turns toward them. "What the hell, Harper?"

"You sayin' you wouldn't've done the same if she'd've asked you?" Harper says.

Ben stands and offers his seat. Harper takes it.

"What choice did she have?" Willow asks.

Ben and Liam step out of the office and return a moment later with some folding chairs.

"You should've tried to convince her she was being paranoid and irrational," Zoey says.

"I did."

Everyone is seated now.

"Not hard enough."

"I tried so hard. But she was . . . she was so traumatized that she couldn't be reasoned with. She was going to do it either way. I felt like I had to help her."

Zoey says, "You should've gotten us involved."

"She didn't want that."

"Or at least told us afterward," Zoey says. "You've let us live all this time thinking . . . she was . . . Not knowing what to think."

"That part *was* cold," Olivia says.

Willow says, "I just can't get over she was that little kid from that Disney show."

"Look," Harper says. "I did the best I could for my best friend. You don't like it, don't be my best friend. All I did was what she asked me to do."

"I understand why you did it," Liam says. "I don't blame you. None of that matters now anyway. All that matters is finding her, getting her back. Do you know where she went?"

Harper shakes her head. "No idea."

"She didn't say anything that might help us find her?" he says.

"I don't think she knew where she was going at that point."

"You've got to have some idea," he says.

"Do *you*?"

"No, but evidently I didn't know her nearly as well as you did."

Blade walks in. "See y'all got the band back together. Feels like a fuckin' *Friends* episode. Apart from the two black people and all."

Zoey says, "Can y'all believe she was Hillary York? I knew there was something special about her, some . . . quality. And she was so pretty."

"I can't get over what that sick prick did to her," Liam says. "Are we sure he doesn't have her? God, I want some time alone in a room with him."

"He's a monster," Zoey says. "I can't believe she was ever with him."

"He needs to be put down like a rabid dog," Liam says.

Blade says, "He wantin' to *Old Yeller* his ass."

"Thing is . . ." Olivia says, "if she wanted to come back, she could have. Wherever she is she's where she wants to be. Shouldn't we respect her wishes and not try to find her?"

"We've got to try," Liam says. "Got to let her know how missed she is, how safe she would be here. If she still wants to stay away . . . then we leave her alone."

"What can we do to help y'all find her?" Harper asks.

Blade says, "Any of y'all know where she is?"

They all indicate they don't.

"Any of y'all have any information about where she *might* be?"

Same response.

"Then what y'all can *do* is get on up outta here and let us do our jobs. We won't be needin' any help from the Scooby gang at this time, but we'll call y'all if we do."

48

———

"That was fun," Blade says when they're gone. "Liked it better when they didn't know shit."

"Bobby Doll with Ashlynn and Alana?" I ask.

"No," she says, her voice rich with sarcasm. "Was I supposed to wait until he got there before leaving?"

Bobby Doll was in the system with us when we were kids. Over the years, Blade and I had helped him out more than a few times. He has sociopathic tendencies and is good with a gun. Anyone tries to get to Ashlynn or Alana he'll make a mess of them.

"You believe them?" Blade asks.

I shrug.

"Really think Harper didn't tell any of them until now?"

"Their surprise and anger and sense of betrayal seemed genuine."

"Maybe," she says. "But none of 'em have any clue where she might be now."

"No one in her previous life knew she was here," I say.

"Maybe."

"Clyde Brousard dropped by this morning," I say.

"Yeah?"

"Owens is out of town—on a South African safari."

She does a spit take. "The fuck? White people, am I right?"

"You're right," I say. "Says he has some time on his hands so he'll see what he can do about Dimitri. Said for us to concentrate on keepin' Ashlynn and Alana safe."

A wide smile spreads across her face.

"What?" I ask.

"You know why he's doin' it," she says.

"He's a good guy," I say. "He cares for Alana."

"Yeah, okay, maybe, but the real reason is he's got a thing for your girl. I can see it in his eyes. Bet he was disappointed as fuck that I wasn't here this morning. He's hopin' to *Chasing Amy* my ass."

"Yeah, I'm sure that's it," I say.

"Mark my words."

"Do you think we should move Ashlynn and Alana to Heather's condo?"

She nods. "Probably. Be way safer than your shitty little apartment."

"Okay. I'll call her. Oh, and I think I might know a way to find Brook . . . but we're gonna need a domestic abuse victim."

49

———

The waning moon is a pale plop of impressionist paint in the cloudy night sky.

Lexi, looking like she's been in a bar fight, is standing in the parking lot of the Bay Breeze motel. Her teased hair, heavy makeup, and cheap, revealing clothes make her look like a cross between a line dancer at a country bar or a bargain basement sex worker.

Her appearance fits nicely with the Bay Breeze—an old, roadside, mom and pop motel with only ten rooms that can be rented by the day, month, or hour. It's one of only a few non-chain motels left in the area and is located in a sketchy stretch of 15th Street between an all-night tattoo parlor and a bar in a 70s-era convenient store building that's on at least its twelfth name change.

She's wired up and waiting.

We're parked across the street in a pop-up pizza joint inside an old Waffle Shop building.

Earlier in the evening she had called a local domestic abuse hotline and pleaded for help. We're hoping the angels coming to her rescue are the same ones Todd Johns saw the night he dropped the bridesmaids off at the hotel.

"They don't show soon," she whispers into her mic, "I'm gonna be propositioned or run off by the police. Or have my feelings hurt because I don't get propositioned."

We can hear her, but she can't hear us. The microscopic mic we wired her up with transmits but doesn't receive, and she has no earpiece because they're too easy to spot.

Earlier in the afternoon we had moved Ashlynn and Alana into Heather's condo in Flamingo South on the west end of Thomas Drive. Clyde is there with them now.

Lexi says, "Hey, Luc, if they don't show, we should get a room for an hour."

"If y'all do," Blade says, "whatcha'll gonna do with the other fifty-eight minutes?"

I laugh.

"Actually," she says, "there's an extra room at Heather's condo y'all can use. Sure that'll go over real well."

Across the street, a white van pulls into the parking lot and stops next to Lexi.

"Vicky?" the older woman in the driver's seat says.

"Yeah," Lexi says with more southern drawl than I would've thought her capable of.

"Hop in?"

"Where're y'all taking me?"

"Can't tell you that," she say. "It's for security purposes. Just like leaving everything behind. No phone. No devices. No credit or debit cards. Nothing but your driver's license and any cash you want to take."

"But you don't need any cash," the woman in the passenger seat says.

"Come on," the woman in the driver's seat says. "We've got to go. I know it's scary. But this is your best chance of a new life without abuse. You can do it, but we've got to do it now."

"Yeah, okay," Lexi says.

She moves around the other side of the van and gets in.

I crank my car.

When the van pulls out into traffic on 15th I wait a beat then follow.

They are in the far right lane headed east at about fifty miles per hour. We're about ten car lengths behind them.

"I been thinkin' 'bout what you said," Blade says.

"Yeah?" I ask, wondering about which of the many things I've said to her she's referring to.

"Yeah. Even if I can't forgive her and let it go . . . I'd like to at least explain to Rush why I did what I did."

"That'd probably be good for both of you," I say.

"But I can't," she says. "I pull her number up on my phone and I just can't make myself make the call."

"Maybe in time," I say.

"Maybe you could do it for me."

"Sure," I say. "Hand me your phone."

"*Now*? While you're drivin' *and* tailin' someone?"

"Why not?"

"Well, shit, okay," she says. "What're you gonna tell her?"

"I'll put it on speaker so you can hear everything," I say.

The white van continues east on 15th past Harrison and MLK.

Traffic is light and I lay back even more, falling to fifteen car lengths or more and switching lanes.

"Don't get too fancy and lose them," she says.

She then pulls out her phone, pulls Rush's number up, and hands it to me.

I press the *call* button and look back at the road.

"*Hey*," Rush says.

There is great warmth in her voice and I'm reminded that her phone showed that Blade was calling.

"Rush, it's Burke," I say.

"Oh. Hey. Wait. What happened? What's wrong? Is she hurt?"

I mute the phone for a moment and say to Blade, "She's obviously still open to you—she answered your call—even after how you acted. She clearly cares very deeply about you too."

"Luc? Luc, are you there?"

"Sorry," I say when I unmute the phone. "I'm here. Blade is fine—except for feeling bad about how she treated you. She's right here and wants to apologize to you."

Blade's eyes grow wide in surprise and then narrow in anger.

"Blade?" Rush says. "Are you there? Is that you?"

"I'm here," she says, her voice tense and flat.

"I'm so, so sorry for how I betrayed you. I . . ."

"I . . ." Blade says. "I . . . overreacted. I's wrong to test you like that. Burke says I have trust issues and he may be right. Anyway, I gotta go. We tailin' some lezzes in a van who get people like you away from people like me."

She ends the call before Rush can respond.

"I'm'a get your ass for that," she says to me.

"What?" I say, trying to suppress a smile. "You said you needed help making the call, so I helped you make the call."

"Okay," she says, nodding to herself. "I'm gonna help you right back. You just wait."

The van takes a right on East Avenue.

I pass East in case they're watching us, pull into the old convenience store, wait a moment, pull up and glance down East, then follow.

It's harder to follow them and not be noticed on the smaller side streets, so I give it even more distance.

They lead us into Millville, to a tiny clapboard house across from the cemetery.

We pull up and park on the street a few houses down and jump out of the car.

Sneaking up toward the property as they exit the van, cross the small yard, and climb the steps to the porch, we are right behind them as they enter the house and follow them inside.

50

"What the—" one of the ladies says.

"Call the—" the other one says.

Within moments Blade and I have taken their phones and weapons.

I think of Todd John's descriptions of these old ladies in the idling van outside of the hotel the night of Brook's disappearance. One does look like a grandma and the other more like a grandpa.

As if an old married couple who looks more and more alike over the years, they strongly resemble one another. They're roughly the same height and weight and size. Both have short gray hair. Both wear glasses. But Grandpa is slightly more masculine and her hair is a dark gray whereas Grandma's is nearly white. Grandma is dressed more femininely and colorfully and is wearing earrings and a hint of makeup. The thick plastic frames of her glasses are a bright aqua-blue whereas Grandpa's are Buddy Holly-black. Grandpa is wearing white work pants and a white t-shirt with a black Buddha head on the front.

"You good?" I ask Lexi.

She nods and steps over beside me.

"You're with them?" Grandma asks.

"What the hell's goin on here?" Grandpa says.

"We're not gonna hurt you," I say. "We're investigators looking for someone just to make sure she's okay. That's it."

I pull out my license and show it to them.

"Told you," Grandpa says.

"Told her what?" Blade asks.

She doesn't respond.

"What did you tell her?"

"That a certain client was going to be trouble—and here y'all are."

"Y'all picked up Brooklyn Hill outside of a hotel at the beach about a year ago," I say. "We just want to make sure she's okay. If she is and wants to stay where she is we'll walk away. If she's not we'll help her. That's it."

"You can beat us, torture us, kill us," Grandpa says. "We won't tell you anything. Not about anyone."

I pull out my phone and text Pete the address.

"'Course you couldn't tell us if we kill you," Blade says.

"We understand your position," I say. "And we appreciate what y'all are doing. We do. We're in the same business. All we're trying to do is make sure she's okay."

"Who're you working for?" Grandma says. "Her ex?"

Shit. "Well, technically, but . . . we're not finding her for him. We're not going to tell him where she is or—"

"Sure," Grandpa says. "We'll just take your word for that. No problem. She's at 177 Suck My Dick Lane."

"Grandpa's feisty," Blade says. "I like it."

"Even if we wanted to help you," Grandma says.

"Which we don't," Grandpa adds.

"Which we don't," Grandma continues, "we wouldn't be able to. We have no idea where anyone is. It's one of our many safety protocols."

"To keep people like you from getting any information from us," Grandpa says. "We have none to give."

"Each depot of our little underground railroad knows nothing about any of the others," Grandma says.

"You think you're the first to do this?" Grandpa says. "We get threatened and assaulted all the time. Only way this works is us not having any info to give."

There's a knock on the front door, and I step over and let Pete in.

After greeting us, he steps over to the two old ladies.

"I'm Pete Anderson," he says, holding up his badge and ID. "I'm with the Bay County Sheriff's Office. I'm looking for Brooklyn Hill. I can assure you no harm will come to her. I only want to verify she is safe and well. It's in your interest and hers to help me. Lexi here works for the department of corrections and Burke and Blade are well respected PIs I've known for most of my life. No one here will do anything but help Ms. Hill. If she is safe and happy where she is and wants to stay then that's what she'll do. We just need to make sure that's the case."

"We actually believe you," Grandpa says, "but it doesn't change the fact that we have no idea whatsoever where anyone we've ever helped is. We only do local pick ups and bring them to a safe house for a few hours or overnight at most. That's it."

"Who picks them up from you?" he asks.

"We don't know. It's someone different every time. We don't know any of them. We don't know anyone else in the process."

"So you could be part of a human trafficking scheme and you wouldn't know it?" Pete says. "I find that hard to believe."

I say, "We can just wait here for whoever comes to pick up Lexi. Follow this up the chain."

Grandpa shakes his head. "They don't pick her up here. We have a different drop-off point every time and it's not set by us."

"Then we'll go to that with you."

"No, you won't. We haven't even made contact yet. We

always wait to make sure the victim is going to go through with it. And we're not going to now. And even if we had we wouldn't take you to the drop-off point."

"But none of that would help you anyway," Grandma says.

Grandpa jerks her head toward her. "Dot, *no*. Don't."

"What can it hurt?" she says. Turning back to Pete, she lets out a long sigh. "None of that would help you anyway because . . . we never delivered her to the drop-off point. When we woke the next morning after getting her she was gone."

51

"I'm sorry things didn't work out tonight," Lexi is saying, "but it was a brilliant plan. And hey . . . it led to this."

Lexi and I are in a room at the Bay Breeze Motel.

After we dropped Blade off she had said, "I was only half kidding about getting a room at the Breeze."

Getting away from everything for a while and being somewhere no one would ever suspect was nearly as appealing as making love with Lexi in a seedy motel room, so I had driven us directly over here and plopped down my money for a full hour.

We are now lying naked, our bodies entangled in each other's, following a particularly vigorous round of sex.

Her outfit and the room added a different dimension to our already erotically-charged attraction, and our lovemaking was by turns fun and playful, aggressive and intense.

We did a few things we've never done before.

"I like the new stuff," she says. "I liked it all. Glad we played the hits too."

"This was . . . inspired," I say. "Thank you for suggesting it."

"Thank you for asking me to dress up like a dirty little slut."

"My pleasure. Truly."

"That was the real reason for your plan, wasn't it?" she says. "Had nothing to do with finding Brook."

"It was certainly the only part of the plan that worked."

"You really think they didn't know anything?" she asks.

I nod.

"And you believe them about her sneaking away while they slept?"

"Tend to," I say. "She knew what she was doing—had done it before—and had the resources to do it."

"What now?" she asks.

"I'm out of ideas," I say.

"What was Blade talkin' about?"

On our drive back to the office to drop Blade off at her car, she had said the only thing left to do was to pull the pin.

"Involving a last-resort kind of guy. She knows I don't like working with him. Don't think she does either."

"Guy got a name?"

"Yeah, but you don't want to know it."

"Yes, I do."

"Conor Shauns."

"And what does Conor Shauns do?"

"Illegal and unethical shit," I say. "He's a hacker. A dark web guy. He fucks with people's lives for fun. Likes spreading chaos. He's also a vindictive little fucker. I don't trust him not to . . . If he knows he's helpin' find Hillary York . . . no tellin' what he might do. He could let the whole world know where she is."

"Oh. But he probably won't be able to find her anyway, will he?"

I shrug. "Probably not. And even if he does . . . he may not care enough to do anything. Never know with him."

"I don't like that you're getting out of our hot hotel bed of debauchery to go to Heather's condo," she says.

"She won't be there," I say.

"Still."

"We're just borrowing it for a safe house," I say.

"I know, but . . . it keeps her in your life, keeps you . . . beholden to her—just like her paying for the damages at Dave's."

"It's not like that," I say. "She's not like that. She's made it clear there are no strings."

"And you believe her? You've got a lot to learn about women."

"Well," I say, "feel free to teach me what you think I need to know."

"Some other time," she says. "We've got about twenty minutes left in our hour and I want you to fuck me again before we have to leave. And do that new tongue thing again. Certainly don't need to be taught anything about that."

52

"If she used a service like the one you say I doubt anyone can find her," Conor Shauns is saying. "Not even me. But sometimes there's enough of a trace left behind to track. It'll just depend on how they did it and how good they are."

He's a few years younger than us in his early twenties and entered the system as we were aging out of it. We've known him for a while, and though he is a little brother to us in some ways I neither like nor trust him.

"We're in the back room of his computer repair shop and internet cafe on 23rd Street not far from the old mall. The shop is mostly empty—a few booths with computers on them up front, a few shelves with dusty computers and parts lining the walls leading to the sales counter in the back. The room we're in is dark and looks like a computer graveyard.

He's sitting in front of his workstation—a computer desk with a one-of-a-kind system he designed and built and two 27-inch monitors.

"Just need a name," he says, tapping his fingers on his desktop with his idle mouse hand, his impatience obvious.

His stringy blond hair is unkempt and in need of cutting, his pale skin could use a little time in the sun, but it's his eyes that overshadow everything else. They're a light green that doesn't look natural, and they never look directly at you.

"We can't stress enough how confidential this is," I say. "Nobody can know about it. Nobody."

"*Okay, okay*. How many times are you going to tell me that?"

"You're gonna want to tell someone," I say. "But you can't. Not even your priest."

"Don't have a priest," he says. "And I won't tell anyone. I swear. Guys, come on. I won't burn you. You know that."

Through the open curtain, I can see that Conor's shop is empty, and though he on occasion does some repair work I've always believed his business is really just a front.

"Very dangerous people are after her," I say. "If they find her she's dead."

"Got it."

"I'm serious."

"I won't tell anybody."

"She's famous," I say. "And so is her ex. You're gonna want to tell someone. You're gonna want to post something."

"I can keep a fuckin' secret," he says. "Keepin' several right now. A few about famous people."

"Like what?" Blade asks.

He starts to say something but stops himself. "You almost got me. Good try."

I glance at Blade and shake my head. This is not a good idea.

She shoots me a *What choice do we have?* look.

"And it's not just that we don't want you tellin' anyone," I say. "Can you do it without anyone knowing you searched?"

"Huh?"

"If someone is monitoring her info. Can you take a look at it without anyone knowing you did?"

"Oh, for sure. No one will know I was there—not even me since this is so top secret."

"Okay," I say. "We're looking for Hillary York."

"*Really*?" he asks in surprise. "Wow."

"Why wow?" I ask.

"I can tell you right where she is," he says. "I went back to before she changed her name and disappeared the first time and I followed the money. Found where she hid it and traced where she'd been accessing it from and what she'd been spending it on. First in Panama City and now in Tampa."

"Why?" I ask.

"Why what?"

"Why'd you do all that in the first place?"

"'Cause Ward Forester hired me to."

53

———

"**F**uckin' Forester," Blade says. "Can't believe he beat us to her."

We're in the car, rushing back to the office to prepare to head to Tampa. I'm driving and attempting to call Brook again on the number Conor found for her.

I've called her two times before and she hasn't answered. This time I leave a message.

"See if you can get him," I say.

She calls him while I try Brook again.

While I'm waiting for my call to go through Brook beeps in.

"Hey, Hillary," I say. "Thanks so much for calling me back."

When she hears me, Blade closes her phone.

"I got your message," she says.

"What's going on?" she asks. "How did you find me?"

"First, let's make sure you're safe," I say. "Where are you?"

"I can't tell you that," she says.

"That's fine," I say, "but a PI hired by one of Raven's fans has your address in Tampa. Is there somewhere else you can go while we—"

"I'm not at that address," she says.

"Good. That's good. Are you safe?"

"I believe so. Thought I was completely safe until I got your message. Still want to know how you found that address and got this number."

As usual, the traffic on 23rd is heavy, and we catch nearly every light.

"I'll be happy to tell you everything," I say. "I just want to make sure you're safe before we get into all that."

"I'm nowhere near that address in Tampa," she says. "So unless someone's tracking this phone. Actually, let me get rid of this phone and call you back. I'll call you back in a minute."

She ends the call and I tell Blade what she said.

Less than a minute later, Hillary calls back from a different number.

We are still headed west on 23rd Street toward our office but at a slower rate of speed.

"I'm Lucas Burke," I say. "My partner—"

"I know who you are," she says. "It's the only reason I called you back. You two found that missing baby and brought that missing mother and child home. I followed y'all while I was in PC in case I ever needed to hire someone local."

"All we care about is your safety," I say. "We have no other agenda."

I start to put the call on speaker but feel like the connection is so tenuous, the trust between us so fragile I don't want to do anything to scare her off. Since Blade hasn't said anything, she must have come to the same conclusion.

"How did you find me?" she asks. "How do you know who I am?"

I give her a brief account of how we got to this phone call.

"So Harper didn't betray me," she says.

"No. She didn't."

I take a left at Lisenby and drive past the cemetery that was such a big part of our previous case.

"I can't believe you figured out how we did it," she says. "And everyone knows now?"

"At last count everyone but Poppy and Annabeth."

"Makes sense. And tell me again how you got the Tampa address and my phone number."

I tell her.

"Interesting," she says. "And that's what the PI working for Raven's follower has?"

"The address," I say. "Not the number."

"Number doesn't matter anyway," she says. "I just burned that phone."

"You don't seem too concerned that Tip Ripper—or at least his PI—has your address."

"That's not my address," she says. "We set that up in case anyone did what you did."

"Nice," I say. "So glad no one's any closer to finding you."

I take a right onto 15th and west toward our office.

"Really?" she asks. "I thought that's what you were trying to do."

"We're just trying to confirm you are where you want to be doing what you want to be doing," I say.

"Certainly can't say that," she says. "I miss Liam and Harper and the others. I miss my life—at least the one I had in Panama City."

"But no one has you imprisoned or is controlling you in any way."

"Just my fears and neuroses."

"As you can imagine I'd rather confirm that you're okay face to face," I say. "Someone could have a gun to your head making you say the things you're saying."

"Yeah, I guess they could, but they're not. *I'm* the only one who holds a gun to my head these days."

"If someone is with you or you're in trouble or danger in any way say, 'You'll never ever find me, so give up now.'"

"No one has me," she says. "I'm safe."

"Would you be willing to meet with us?" I say. "We'll come anywhere you like."

"I overreacted," she says. "I freaked out. I regret what I did. Especially now that everyone knows."

"They care for you," I say, "and understand why you did what you did. They just want you safe. Well, Liam wants you back and believes your safest and best life is with him, but . . ."

She doesn't say anything.

After a few moments, I say, "You still there?"

"I'm here."

"We'd really like to meet with you just to know for sure you're okay. It can be anywhere. You could pick a city you don't live in. We could go to that city. You could tell us at the last second where you want to meet. You could come with body-guards. You could make sure we're alone and—"

"Let me think about everything," she says. "I'll call you back."

She ends the call before I can say anything.

When I drop my phone onto the seat, Blade says, "Well?"

"Says she's safe. The Tampa address and that phone number were in case anyone tried to do what Conor did."

"*Daa-umn*. Girl's good."

"Says she regrets what she did—especially now that everyone knows."

"She willin' to meet with us?" she asks.

"Not sure. She is familiar with some of our work, followed a few cases when she lived in PC. Said she needed to think and would call me back."

"Think we'll ever hear from her again?"

"I'd say fifty-fifty."

"After all the shit we been through and your ass is still an optimist."

"You think fifty-fifty is optimistic?"

"I think we never hearin' from the bitch again."

We pull into the parking lot of our building but don't get out.

"If we don't . . ." I say.

"Say we let this one go," she says. "Don't know what else we could do to find her."

I nod. "Yeah. Unless we get something else to go on . . . have no idea what a next move would be."

She nods. "Okay."

I turn the car off and we're about to get out when my phone rings.

It's Hillary.

"I'd like to talk to them," she says.

"Who?" I ask.

"Liam, Harper, and the others. Try to explain—since they already know. Could you help me set up a sit-down with them? You could confirm I'm safe—at least from everyone but myself —at the same time."

54

———————

"I don't expect you to understand," Hillary is saying, "but I wanted to try to explain."

We are in the conference room of Coastal Connections, a real estate agency that's closed for renovations. It's located on the west end of the beach.

Hillary is standing at the head of the long wooden table, Blade, Ben, and I near the door. The others are seated at the chairs around the table—Harper, Zoey, Willow, Olivia, Poppy, Annabeth, and Liam. Harper and Liam are seated closest to Hillary.

"But first let me say two things," she says. "I'm sorry for what my actions have put you through. You especially, Liam. You didn't deserve that. And I want you to know that if you had been indicted I would have come back and explained everything to the DA."

Liam nods and smiles. "It's okay," he says. "Everything is okay. We understand and we love you."

Most of the bridesmaids nod and express their agreement with Liam's sentiments.

"The thing to remember is . . . this happened—or at least

started happening when I was a kid. My mom was dead and my dad wasn't around. And this malevolent monster moved in and began a systematic campaign of psychological warfare on me. He was charming and sweet. He was edgy and mysterious. He was this huge rock star and he . . . he only wanted me. No groupies. No friends. Just me. He met my every need. He took such good care of me. Indulged me like I had never been indulged before. But he also began the process of isolating me from everyone else. Testing me, making me prove my love and commitment to him. He took his time. He knew what he was doing and how to do. He was an accomplished and highly skilled predator. And over the course of years he dismantled me, took me apart piece by piece and rebuilt me into his . . . I'm not sure what I even was. His child. His slave. His property. His victim. His fuck doll. His. I was his. And he abused and degraded and terrorized me for years. To say I still have PTSD is an understatement. To say I'm paranoid and fearful and fucked up doesn't even begin to cover it. All of this began when I was a child. And my counselor says anytime I get anxious or scared or feel threatened I revert back to that age. In many ways I stopped developing at fourteen when he sank his talons into me. I'm stunted. I . . . What I did . . . the way I overreacted wasn't about any of you. Especially you, Liam. I know now you were just being protective and caring, but it felt like control and domination and I thought *this* is how it begins. It's starting all over again. And I . . . I just lost it. I reverted back to . . . My instincts and programing and lizard brain kicked in and I . . . I did what I do. Fight or flight? I flew. It had nothing to do with any of you. Seeing that Raven fanboy at Newby's just solidified everything and confirmed I was right to run. I don't expect you to understand or forgive me, but . . . since you now know I wanted to at least try to explain."

"We do understand," Liam says. "And there's nothing to forgive. Nothing at all."

Willow says, "We're just so sorry you went through all that. What an unbelievable nightmare."

Hillary says, "It was systematic and prolonged torture."

"If you could have just trusted us enough to tell us we could've helped you," Zoey says. Her tone is harsher than the others and filled with hurt, betrayal, and anger. In spite of that she still sounds like she's talking to kindergartners. "In every way. Not just keeping you safe but with your mental stuff and—"

"Trusting Harper was the single biggest step I've taken since I got out of the prison Raven had me in."

"I'm so honored," Harper says. "And I didn't betray you. Didn't tell anyone."

"You told all of us," Zoey says.

Harper points at me. "*He* figured it out. *I* didn't tell him. *He* told me."

"But you told us," Zoey says. "He didn't."

"Only after he knew and it was going to come out. I wanted Liam to hear it from me."

"Well, he did," Zoey says. "We all did."

Liam says to Hillary, "All that matters is that you're safe, that you're okay. That we have you back."

I can tell from Hillary's reaction that he nor the group have her back, but she recovers and doesn't say anything.

Olivia says, "I just want to say that you are a survivor, that you are far stronger and more resilient than you give yourself credit for. And I admire how you took back control of your life and did what you had to do."

"Thank you," Hillary says. "That means a lot."

"I couldn't agree more," Poppy says.

"Another entire aspect of this whole thing," Hillary says. "I'm not making excuses. I'm trying to explain to you why I did what I did to you. But another . . . element in all of this is that both Raven and his rabid fans have said many times that they intend to kill me. I was getting death threats every day before I . . . back when I was still Hillary."

"Who are you now?" Zoey asks.

Hillary flinches a little and looks at her, shaking her head and narrowing her eyes. "I . . . I can't . . . It doesn't matter."

"So you still don't trust us," Zoey says.

"I'll tell you who I am," she says. "I'm that same scared lost little orphaned fourteen-year-old I was when Raven swooped in and dragged me to hell. Anyway . . . like I said . . . I don't expect you to forgive me, but I was hoping you might understand a little better if I explained it."

"We do," Liam says.

"I'm sure you all have plenty you'd like to say to me and probably have all kinds of questions, but . . . I'm not sure how much I have left in me tonight and . . . I still want to talk to Liam alone if that's okay."

"Of course," Liam says. "Everyone get a hug and welcome Brook back and . . . There will be plenty of time later for . . . to talk more."

55

"Want us to stay?" I ask.

Hillary shakes her head.

Blade and Liam are in the parking lot taking a look around and making sure everyone gets to their vehicle safely.

Hillary and I are alone in the conference room.

"I'm gonna have a quick chat with Liam and then I'll be gone again."

"We can hang around until you do and escort you to where you're going."

"I have a driver and a bodyguard," she says. "They'll make sure I'm good."

I nod. "Okay. Anything else we can do?"

She shakes her head. "Thank you for . . . not just what you've done but the way you've done it. You all are good people, and I won't ever forget what you've done for me."

"You have my number," I say. "Hold onto it. You ever need us, don't hesitate to call."

"Don't be surprised if I call you sometime," she says. "You

have really impressed me, and if I need something you'll be my first call."

"I hope we will be," I say.

She looks at me and nods and an awkward moment passes between us.

"I wanted to say . . . how sorry I am for everything you went through," I say. "Blade and I both know what it's like to be young, vulnerable orphans. The worst people on the planet are the ones who prey on . . . children."

"I know you do. I can tell. And it . . . it helps. I . . . It's so . . . You have no idea how lucky you are to have found each other."

Actually, we do, but I don't feel the need to say so.

"If I had found someone back then . . ." she says and lets it hang in the air like an unanswered prayer.

"I wish you had."

"Well, anyway, trying to heal and recover and do better moving forward."

"We don't have to . . ." I say. "Don't just call us if you have work for us. You can call us anytime for anything. We can be your . . . friends instead of employees."

She seems taken aback. "That's . . . Thank you. I really . . . I only have employees. I could use some friends."

"I know you can only know this over time, but you can trust us. We don't care about the fame or the money or any of that shit."

She grabs me and hugs me.

We are still hugging when Liam and Blade walk back in.

56

"That could've gone worse," Blade is saying.

We are driving back to Heather's condo to relieve Clyde Brousard.

The night is bright with a big moon and a billion blinking stars.

Since it's off season and the snowbirds aren't out at night, we take Front Beach with the windows down to hear the surf.

I nod and don't add that it could've gone better.

"What is it?" she asks.

"I feel bad," I say. "For . . . well, all of them. Feel bad for Hillary, obviously. She's . . ."

"Fucked," Blade offers.

"Yeah. But I feel bad for Liam too. And the others, but especially Liam."

"Why?"

"He thinks she's back."

"Not for long," she says. "I'm sure she gonna break it to him gently, but she gonna break it to him."

Occasionally, around and in between the mammoth condos

and hotels a small sliver of the beach can be seen, the moon's reflection bouncing on the gentle rocking waters of the Gulf.

"Seemed like the others thought she was back too," I say.

"She'll never be back," she says. "Anywhere."

I nod. "I'm saddest of all for that little fourteen-year-old girl she can't go back to."

"Look, I get it," she says, "but . . . and I'm sure plenty of people can say the same shit about us. We can't go back to when we had parents and families. But . . . think about the case. It's a good result—as good as it gets. We found the missing person. She's alive and well and safe. We helped Ben out. We kept an innocent man from being wrongly indicted. It's a good result. Results don't get any better. Now, let's concentrate on protecting Ashlynn and Alana and dismantling Dimitri's life."

57

———

"How'd it go?" Clyde asks.

"Could've gone worse," Blade says.

I add, "Seemed pretty cathartic."

"Everything was quiet here," he says. "That little girl is too much, man. So cute and sweet. And so damn funny."

"Can't tell you how much we appreciate this," I say.

"Happy to help."

"We know why you doin' it," Blade says and winks at him. "And it's all good."

He's clearly confused, but I remember her saying he was helping us because he has a thing for her.

There's an awkward beat before he says, "Not making much headway with the Dimitri situation. I was tryin' to get a little Russian mobster civil war going, but no luck so far. Still working on it though."

"And we know why," Blade says and winks again.

Ignoring her, he says, "If that doesn't work soon I'll try something else. Like to have this shit wrapped before Logan gets back."

"Let us know what we can do to help," I say. "And thank you again for everything you're doing. We appreciate it more than you'll ever know."

58

———————

I'm standing in the doorway to the master bedroom watching Alana sleep and feeling grateful when Ashlynn walks up beside me.

"How long can we do this?" she asks.

"As long as it takes."

She shakes her head. "I can't keep living off y'all," she says. "Can't have everyone stopping their lives to take care of us."

"We're happy to do it," I say. "Keepin' our family safe matters more than anything else we do."

"How much longer do you think it'll be?"

"Don't know for sure. It's early days."

"I'm . . . gettin' a little stir crazy. Not sure how much longer I can do this."

"Please just be patient," I say. "We'll get this resolved, but this is the best way to keep you and Alana safe until we do."

"What if I . . . I was thinking Alana and I could just move to another town."

My heart sinks into my stomach.

The thought of losing them—especially Alana—sends tremors of loss and anxiety down my spine.

"Please, no," I say. "We need to stay together. Our family is—"

"But we're not family, are we?"

"Yes, we are," I say. "We absolutely are. I'd do anything for you and Alana. You are my sister. She is my niece. I love y'all with all my heart. Please."

She doesn't say anything.

"Starting over in a new town with no support system would be extremely difficult," I say. "Finding someone to keep Alana while you work will be so hard—and you'd never find anyone who loves her as much as we do, who would take as good care of her as we do."

"I know. And I know you'd miss her, but . . . we could visit and FaceTime and stuff."

"It'd be dangerous too," I say. "Dimitri could track you wherever you go. Please. I'm begging you not to do it."

"I haven't made any final decisions or anything," she says. "Just thinking about it."

59

"She's gone," Liam is saying.

His call has awakened me out of a deep sleep.

I'm disoriented, and it takes me a moment to realize where I am.

I'm on the couch in Heather's condo. I look around at the dim unit. Both bedroom doors are closed—the master with Ashlynn and Alana in it and the kids' room with Blade in it.

I pull my phone back from my ear and look at the time. It's a little after three in the morning.

"Something's wrong though," he says. "She didn't just run again. I think someone has her."

"What makes you think that?"

"How soon can you get to my place?"

"Fifteen minutes," I say.

"Please hurry."

60

"I woke up and she was gone," Liam is saying. "She would't just run away like that. Not again. Not after last time."

We're in his apartment on Back Beach. He moved in here after he sold his home to pay to find Brook and for potential legal fees.

I'm here alone, having left Blade at the condo to guard Ashlynn and Alana.

"Tell me what happened after we left the real estate office."

"We talked for a few minutes there and then went for a ride," he says. "She was trying to tell me she wasn't coming back, that this was goodbye. I begged her for the chance to change her mind. Told her the least she could do was hear me out. She said she owed me that at least. We decided to go for a drive and a walk along the beach. She told her driver and body-guard to go get something to eat and she'd call them later. We talked and talked. Well, mostly I talked, begging and pleading with her to let me take care of her and protect her from Raven and the rest. She was very gentle and kind, but it was still a *no*. But even still we wound up back here and she agreed to spend one last night with me. She called her driver and security guard and dismissed them. Told them she'd call them when she was ready tomorrow. We had a very nice time. She was so sweet and kind. I tried to stay up, to make the night last as long as it could, but . . . I guess I fell asleep. When I woke up around a little before three she was gone. I called her driver and security guard. It was obvious I woke them up. They didn't know anything about it. They're on their way over here now. I don't think she left on her own."

"How'd you have their number?" I ask.

"Brook gave it to me earlier in the evening in case something happened to her."

"Any sign of forced entry?"

He shakes his head.

"Any signs of violence or—"

"No and I know how it sounds, but I don't think she just left again. I really don't. And if she was going to, wouldn't she have called her driver and security guard?"

"Did she leave anything behind or—"

"No, but she didn't have much to begin with."

"Let's look around and we'll talk to the driver and bodyguard when they get here."

As we look around, I call Hillary's number—or at least the last number she called me from.

It rings several times then goes to a generic automated voicemail.

I call her several more times as I look around the house and the area around his apartment and get the same result.

Since her phone is still on and receiving calls it can be traced.

I call Pete, wake him up, tell him what's going on, and ask if he can get a location on the phone.

"No promises," he says, "but I'll see what I can do."

By the time we finish the search of the house and the property, the driver and bodyguard have arrived.

I walk out to meet them in the parking lot and Liam follows me.

"Can you give us a minute?" I ask him.

"I guess," he says and reluctantly walks back inside.

I don't know the driver very well, but I've worked with the bodyguard before. He's who I talk to.

"I don't care if you helped her get away," I say. "That's what you're supposed to do, and when I left her earlier tonight that's what I thought you were doing. But I need to know whether you did or not so I don't waste a lot of time and resources and wake up the wrong people. I won't tell anyone anything. I just need to know."

"Burke, I swear we were sound asleep—both of us—when dude called. We were just trying to get a little shut-eye before we had to pick her up in the morning. Haven't seen her since she left with him after the meeting tonight. Got no reason to lie. Like you say that's what we were supposed to do. And I'd have no reason to lie to you about it. You have my word."

I'm inclined to believe him.

"Okay."

"Anything we can do to help?" he asks.

"Just let me know if she contacts you or if she gets you to take her somewhere. Don't need the details. Don't want to know where she goes, but that she left on her own volition."

"You got it. And call us if you find her or if we can help in any way."

When they pull away, Liam walks out.

"Where're they going?" he asks. "Why'd you want to talk to them without me?"

"Wanted to make sure they would talk freely," I say. "Wasn't sure if they would in front of you."

"Do they know where she is?"

I shake my head.

"Who do you think has her? What do we do next?"

"Give me a few minutes to figure that out," I say. "I need to make a couple of calls. Why don't you go in and get paper and a pen and write down everything y'all did tonight and everything y'all said. Every single thing you can remember. Something she said or did may be the key to figuring out what happened to her or where she might have gone."

"Seems like busy work to keep me occupied but okay."

I call Blade and fill her in when he's gone.

"Chances are she ran again," she says.

"Hope so, but ..."

"What?"

"No, that's what it looks like but . . . something doesn't feel right. And if she did run, it looks like she didn't use her security team. Why wouldn't she use them?"

"Maybe she drops them like she drops phones."

"Maybe."

"How about Liam?" she asks. "He could've done something to her and is tryin' to set up an alibi."

"I'm watching him closely," I say. "Getting a written statement from him and about to interview him again. But ... I don't think he had anything to do with it."

"Have you checked with Ward?" she asks. "If Liam didn't do it and she didn't run . . . He could definitely get in and out of there without leaving a trace if he wanted to."

As soon as I end the call with her I call Ward.

"The fuck, Burke, it's the middle of the goddamn night."

"I wake you?" I ask.

"You know good and goddamn well you did."

He sounds genuinely drowsy, his mouth dry, his throat hoarse.

"Do you have Hillary?"

"*What*? No. You talk to Conor? The Tampa thing was a dead-end. Why would you think I have her?"

"Did you tell Tip anything?"

"Fuck no. And I'm not goin' to. I just takin' him for all I can get. Creepy little fuck. If I ever do find her—and I want to just to say I did—I sure as shit not gonna tell that little weirdo where she is. Swear man. You have my word. I know my work may not be the most ethical, but my word to you is good. I swear."

"Okay," I say. "Thanks."

"Why'd you call me in the middle of the night to ask me about this? Couldn't wait til morning?"

61

———

I'm about to head back into Liam's apartment when it hits me.

If Liam, Ward, Tip, and the security team had nothing to do with Hillary's disappearance, and I'm pretty sure they didn't, and if she left on her own volition, then it's possible she did what she had done before and asked for Harper's help.

I call Harper.

And wake her up.

"What is it? What's wrong?"

"Is Brook with you?"

"*What*? No."

"Did you pick her up earlier tonight?"

"I haven't seen her since I hugged her goodbye at the real estate office earlier this evening. I've been at home with my husband the rest of the night. Why? What's happened? Is she—?"

"Just tryin' to get a location on her. Go back to—"

"Wait," she says. "I . . . I have two missed calls from her around one. I must've slept through them. I can't believe they didn't wake me up. I wish they would have if she needed me."

She continues to talk, but I don't hear her.

I'm thinking about who Hillary would reach out to next—after being unable to get Harper. I go through the list of bridesmaids. Obviously, it wouldn't be Annabeth. I can't see her helping Hillary sneak away from her brother's house. And she and Poppy probably weren't close enough, so that leaves Willow, Zoey, and Olivia. For a variety of reasons I think it would be Zoey.

"Luc," Harper is saying, "are you there?"

"I've got to go," I say. "I'll let you know something as soon as—"

I break the connection and call Zoey.

She doesn't answer.

When I get her voicemail I leave a message and call her again.

She answers on the second ring.

"Luc?" she says. "Is everything okay?"

Her voice sounds odd, even more strained, uptight, and kindergarten-condescending than usual, but it doesn't sound like she was asleep.

I rush to my car.

"Have you heard from Hillary?"

"Who? Oh, Brook. I'll always think of her as Brook I guess. No, I haven't. Why? We just saw her earlier tonight. I honestly thought that would be the last time we ever saw her. Did she run away again? Figures. Between you and me . . . it's probably better off for all of us if she did. Especially Liam. Bless his poor little heart. All she's ever done is stomp on it."

"You didn't give her a ride somewhere tonight?" I ask.

"A ride?"

"Yeah."

"Why would I give her a—Anyway, no, I didn't. I haven't. And I haven't heard from her. Sorry. I wish I could help you. I really do."

"No one would blame you for helping her get away again," I say. "And if you did . . . I wouldn't ask you where you took her or any details. I just want to make sure she left of her own volition."

"Well, you know she did," she says. "Just like last time. If she *did* leave she only did so because she wanted to. I hope you learned your lesson last time, Mr., and aren't going to waste time searching for someone who doesn't want to be found."

"Okay," I say. "Please let me know if you hear from her. I just want to know she's safe."

"Oh, I'm sure she is," she says. "Just like last time, but I will let you know if I hear anything."

When we end the call I still continue toward her house.

Liam calls.

"Where'd you go?"

"I've got to check on something. I'l be back in a few."

"But—"

Pete beeps in and I switch over to his call.

"All I have so far is which tower it pinged off of most recently," he says. "May have more later, but . . ."

"Which tower?" I ask.

"One over off Brandywine Road."

"Great," I say. "That's exactly where I'm headed. It's the one closest to Zoey Wanamaker's house."

62

———

Zoey's house is located at the end of a cul de sac in an older subdivision off of Brandywine Road just before the Hathaway Bridge. It's small with virtually no yard, crammed in with other homes that look nearly identical.

I park out on the cul de sac in front of her schoolhouse mailbox and jump out.

As I walk up her short driveway, I touch the hood of her car. It's still warm.

I look inside it and see some smears of blood in the passenger's seat.

Her front door is ajar. I knock but walk in without waiting for a response.

"Zoey," I call out.

I step into a home that is quaint and colorful, cheaply furnished and decorated with what looks like art projects she made with her kindergarten class.

"Zoey," I call out again.

She appears from the hallway in a bathrobe with a towel in her hand. Her hair is wet and her skin red and damp.

"It's pretty late for a visit, Mr.," she says.

"Pretty late for a shower too."

"I'm really too tired to talk right now," she says. "Can you come back tomorrow? Or . . . better yet, I'll come by your office in the morning—later this morning."

"Where is Hillary?" I ask.

"You already asked me that," she says. "See previous answer."

"We traced her phone here," I say.

"Okay, you caught me. Boy, are you relentless. You were right. She did call me and I gave her a ride. But remember you said I didn't have to tell you where. She is safe and sound, just wanted to leave again—tonight instead of tomorrow."

"Where is she?" I ask. "Is she okay?"

"I just told you."

"I saw the blood in your car," I say. "The police are on the way. I can help you. Just take me to her. Tell me what happened."

She steps over and collapses into an overstuffed faux leather chair.

After a long sigh she begins to cry softly.

I walk over and stand in front of her.

"Tell me what happened," I say. "Where she is."

"She called me and asked me for a ride. Said she couldn't get Harper to answer her phone. She . . . didn't really even ask, just sort of told me to—to come to the apartment of my ex-fiancé who she stole from me because she couldn't spend another second in the prison of his sad apartment. That's what she said. I was so . . . mad . . . but I went anyway. I was happy to get her as far away from Liam as I could. She never treated him right, was never good to him. Just used him. When she got into my car she didn't even say thank you or—she just started saying how boring he was and how she had only ever been with him because he was safe but how she couldn't breathe in his place, couldn't even wait til morning. Said it was a mistake to come back. Said even the sex she had with him earlier in the night was boring and she only gave him some 'cause she felt so sorry for him. Said she felt bad for all of us. She was so . . . condescending, so . . ."

I step over to the kitchen table, grab a few napkins, and bring them to her.

She creases them and dabs at her eyes with the corners.

"Have you ever just lost it? she asks. "Gone into some kind of state where you weren't exactly yourself anymore?"

"No," I say, "I never have."

"I just lost it. I was already so . . . mad at what she had done —at all the things she had done, taking Liam, leaving us all like that. It was belittling and embarrassing. And she rubbed my face in it, asking me to be in her stupid wedding, go on her stupid bachelorette weekend. Always being the center of attention, always acting as if she's better than us. Then for her to come back into our lives like this and to . . . treat Liam like a . . . have him running after her like a little puppy dog again—only to leave him . . . sneak out in the middle of the night and then to use me, sit in my car and trash him, us, while I'm doing her a fuckin' favor. She actually told me I could have him back now. I couldn't take another . . ."

I wonder how much of what she's saying bears any resemblance to what actually happened and how much is an attempt at justification.

"I had some things from my classroom in my backseat . . ." she continues. "I reached back and felt around and found a brick from the old Jefferson School they tore down. I had gone and gotten a brick for every student in my class, cleaned them, and we painted them together—flowers, butterflies, caterpillars. I made one for my classroom and one for my home. I grabbed it and squeezed it and . . . before I knew what I was doing . . . I hit her in the back the head with it. And I kept hitting her. Swerving all around like a drunk driver. Finally pulled over on the side of the road, leaned over, and opened her door. She just fell out onto the shoulder and I . . . I came around and kept bashing her head in. Her pretty, stupid, mean, dumb-dumb head. I couldn't stop. I didn't stop . . . until her . . . face was gone. Nothing left for Liam to look at. No stupid mouth to condescend to me with."

"Where was that?" I ask. "Where is she now? Is she . . ."

"Dead? Very much so. Guess I'll be an honorary member of Raven LuRue's fan club now that I did what none of them could."

"Where is her body?" I ask.

"Where do you think, Mr. Detective? In my trunk."

63

Pete arrives first.

He had been my first call.

After he cuffs Zoey and places her in the back of his car, we go take a look in her trunk.

With gloved hands, he unlocks and opens it.

The slowly opening trunk lid reveals the crumpled and bloodied body of Hillary York surrounded by various items from Zoey's classroom—a brightly painted wooden easel, construction paper, markers and crayons, bulletin board borders, picture books, Post-it notes, a couple of cubbies, random kid's clothes, a giant spiral-topped pad of chart paper, computer-printed pictures of smiling gapped-tooth kids, and the brick with bloodied flowers and butterflies on it.

The juxtaposition of kid-friendly kindergarten classroom materials with the bloodied, unrecognizable victim of violent murder is as revolting as it is ridiculous.

Because of the condition of the face I wonder for a moment if perhaps the body is that of Harper's instead of Hillary's, but quickly conclude that it's Hillary. Not only had I spoken with Harper earlier and she and Hillary sound nothing alike, but in the time that had passed since Brook disappeared, Harper had put on a few pounds and Hillary had not.

We stand there in silence looking down at the horrific scene before us.

The macabre spectacle has an utterly absurd quality that adds to its disturbing and disgusting effect.

By the time other investigators and the crime scene unit have arrived we still haven't uttered a word. What could either of us possibly say?

64

"**I** keep thinkin' she'd still be alive if we hadn't done anything," I say.

Blade says, "Hard not to see it that way."

It's early afternoon the next day. Blade, Ben, and I are in our office. I spent the morning giving statements and answering questions and feeling guilty as fuck.

When I'm not feeling guilty, I feel sad. When I'm not feeling sad, I feel nothing.

"I don't see it that way at all," Ben says. "You didn't deliver her to her killer. You didn't force her to come back or to go with Liam or to release her bodyguard or to sneak out in the middle of the night or call Zoey to come get her—and that's not to mention all the things she had done to Zoey over the years to build up that level of resentment and rage."

"Who knew a chubby kindergarten teacher could be carrying around that much . . . rage," Blade says.

"I'm serious," Ben says. "Don't take this on yourself. We're talkin' about severely damaged people. Everything was set in motion long before you came along. We know a good bit about

Hillary's trauma, but we know next to nothing about Zoey's. Whatever it is has nothing to do with you."

"You *did* offer to stay with her and protect her ass until she left," Blade says.

"I understand everything y'all are saying, but . . ." I say. "If we hadn't found her, hadn't talked to her, hadn't asked to meet with her, hadn't facilitated the meeting between her and the group . . . she'd still be alive right now."

"Can't argue that," Blade says.

Clyde Brousard appears at the door.

"Come on in and take my seat," Ben says, standing. "I've got a client waiting for me."

The two men pass one another just inside the office, Clyde dwarfing Ben.

"Heard what happened," Clyde says as he sits down next to Blade in one of the client chairs.

His enormous frame is too big for the chair, so he sits sideways, a good deal of him hanging out of it.

Blade says, "White chicks, am I right?"

He laughs.

"Repression is dangerous shit," Blade says. "Why I let all my shit out all the time."

"We should've been there," I say.

"Can't be everywhere all the time," he says.

"We had a string of good results to our cases," Blade says. "But not anymore."

Clyde says, "My daddy used to say every piece can't be a masterpiece."

"That's 'cause he didn't know me," she says. "All my pieces are masterpieces."

We all fall quiet a moment.

Eventually, Clyde says, "Hate to pile on . . . but . . . Logan's back in town. Got to pull off the Russian thing for a while.

Really haven't gotten anywhere with it yet. And . . . he wants to see you. Got a job for you."

"Okay," I say. "I'll get around to see him as soon as I can. And we appreciate you doing all you did about Dimitri."

"Ain't done yet. Just got to pull back for a while. Can still help watch that little girl sometimes."

Blade lets out a sigh. "Just keeps comin'. Never stops."

"And neither do we," I say. "Neither do we."

65

———

Friends of Brooklyn Hill mourn together at the same place the food and flowers are dropped off—Liam's apartment.

I stop by that evening.

So far there is no media camped out front, but it won't be long until they arrive. Raven released a statement earlier today saying his nightmare is finally over and the lies and false accusations can now stop. He went on to say that she got what she deserved and he wished he could've been there to see it. He finished by offering a large reward for crime scene or autopsy photos.

Inside, I can't help but notice that most of those gathered were also friends of Zoey Wanamaker, though she is neither mentioned nor mourned.

Olivia shakes my hand and says, "It's good of you to come by."

She nods to the HoneyBaked Ham I had grabbed on the way over and adds, "You can put that in the kitchen and sign the guestbook."

I encounter and hug and offer condolences to most of the bridesmaids as I make my way to the kitchen.

No one seems to blame me for what happened or bear me any ill will, which surprises me.

I find Liam and Harper in the kitchen.

Their eyes are red, their faces puffy and splotchy, tears intermittently rolling down their cheeks.

"Thank you," Liam says when I place the ham on the counter with the other food.

I hug them both. "I'm so sorry."

Harper says, "I still just can't believe it. My . . . mind can't even acknowledge it might be true."

Liam nods, "Yeah, I can't believe Brook is really gone, but . . . what I really can't believe is that Zoey . . . *Zoey* could . . ." He shakes his head. "It's just not possible."

"Guess we can never know what's truly inside another person," Harper says.

Earlier in the day at different times both Lexi and Heather had reached out to me, and though I appreciated their care and concern I'm not ready to see either of them yet.

Liam says, "I wish I'd've never tried to find her, that I'd've said goodbye after our gathering last night and not pressured her to go with me. Hell, I wish I'd've never made that call the night of her bachelorette party. If I hadn't . . . she'd still be alive."

"I wish I had never agreed to help her run away," Harper says. "If I hadn't done that . . . she'd still be alive."

"Neither of you are responsible in any way for what happened," I say. "Don't take that guilt on. None of this is your fault. And even if you had made other choices, taken other paths, there's no guarantee things would've worked out any differently."

66

———

Even though I haven't slept in nearly forty hours and I'm having a hard time keeping my eyes open, I play several games of Pop the Pig, Candy Land, and Barbies with Alana that night—and doing so actually brings me joy and heals my heart.

"I love you so much," I whisper to Alana as I hug her.

"Love you too, now let's play," she says.

Eventually, after she and Ashlynn go to bed, I fall asleep on the couch.

I had wanted to open Kaylee's case file and work on it some before bed, but I was out before I could even lift it off the table.

My restless sleep is deep and haunted.

I dream absurd and outlandish narratives, mostly featuring Hillary, Zoey, Harper, and, eventually, a grownup version of Alana, who in my dreams is the same age as the others.

I'm begging and pleading for her not to go out with the others for the bachelorette weekend. I tell her to stay home and play Pop the Pig and Candy Land with me instead, but she laughs at such an inane suggestion and assures me she'll be all right.

When I open my eyes the next morning and see a note with my name on it propped against a small stack of books next to Kaylee's case file on the coffee table I know they are gone.

I sit up quickly, grab the note, unfold the piece of paper, and, squinting against the morning sunlight streaming in the sliding glass door of the balcony, read what Ashlynn as written.

Dear Luc,

I'm sorry but I have to go. I have to get away from this place, from that man. I'm going to make a fresh start for me and Alana. Please understand. Please let us go. I've picked up a few tricks from you and Blade over the years and may be harder to find than you think, but I'm asking you, begging you, not to look for us. Please. Please let us go. This is what I want. This is what I need. Even if you find us I won't come back with you, so it would be a waste of time anyway. Thank you for all you've done. You have been such a great brother to me and a father figure and friend to Alana. I was wrong when I said we weren't family. You are about all the family we have in the world. I love you and I'll always be grateful to you for all you've done for me but especially for Alana. This isn't goodbye forever. We'll see you again one day. I promise.

Love always,

Ashlynn

It's 1940's Panama City, Florida. The world is at war, and the growing panhandle paradise is doing its part. Tyndall Field is training pilots. Wainwright Shipyard is building battleships. The Naval Section Base is protecting vessels in the Gulf. The Dixie Sherman Hotel is hosting celebrities such as Clark Gable. Harry Lewis, a wealthy banker, is running for mayor, unaware his wife is running for her life.

With a secret to hide and a husband running for mayor in a city exploding and expanding like no other time in history, Lauren doesn't want trouble, but she's about to get a double-barrel full of it. Only one man can help her, and though it might destroy him, he doesn't mind. Better to die than be the walking wounded.

Get The Big Goodbye and begin your fun, romantic, and mysterious journey with Jimmy and Lauren today!

"Lister's hard-edged prose ranks with the best of contemporary noir fiction." *Publisher's Weekly* **Starred Review**

ALSO BY MICHAEL LISTER

(John Jordan Novels)

Power in the Blood

Blood of the Lamb

The Body and the Blood

Double Exposure

Blood Sacrifice

Rivers to Blood

Burnt Offerings

Innocent Blood
(Special Introduction by Michael Connelly)

Separation Anxiety

Blood Money

Blood Moon

Thunder Beach

Blood Cries

A Certain Retribution

Blood Oath

Blood Work

Cold Blood

Blood Betrayal

Blood Shot

Blood Ties

Blood Stone

Blood Trail

Bloodshed

Blue Blood

And the Sea Became Blood

The Blood-Dimmed Tide

Blood and Sand

A John Jordan Christmas

Blood Lure

Blood Pathogen

Beneath a Blood-Red Sky

Out for Blood

What Child is This?

Blood Reckoning

(Burke and Blade Mystery Thrillers)

The Night Of

The Night in Question

All Night Long

(Jimmy Riley Novels)

The Girl Who Said Goodbye

The Girl in the Grave

The Girl at the End of the Long Dark Night

The Girl Who Cried Blood Tears

The Girl Who Blew Up the World

(Merrick McKnight / Reggie Summers Novels)

Thunder Beach

A Certain Retribution

Blood Oath

Blood Shot

(Remington James Novels)

Double Exposure

(includes intro by Michael Connelly)

Separation Anxiety

Blood Shot

(Sam Michaels / Daniel Davis Novels)

Burnt Offerings

Blood Oath

Cold Blood

Blood Shot

(Love Stories)

Carrie's Gift

(Short Story Collections)

North Florida Noir

Florida Heat Wave

Delta Blues

Another Quiet Night in Desperation

(The Meaning Series)

Meaning Every Moment

The Meaning of Life in Movies

Sign up for Michael's newsletter by clicking here or go to www.MichaelLister.com and receive a free book.

www.ingramcontent.com/pod-product-compliance
Lightning Source LLC
Chambersburg PA
CBHW050842190726
48286CB00007B/2191